JOURNEY
of the
MESSIAH

THE AWAKENING

HARRY L. WHITT

WESTBOW
PRESS®
A DIVISION OF THOMAS NELSON
& ZONDERVAN

WestBow Press books may be ordered through booksellers or by contacting:

WestBow Press
A Division of Thomas Nelson & Zondervan
1663 Liberty Drive
Bloomington, IN 47403
www.westbowpress.com
844-714-3454

Because of the dynamic nature of the Internet, any web addresses or links contained in this book may have changed since publication and may no longer be valid. The views expressed in this work are solely those of the author and do not necessarily reflect the views of the publisher, and the publisher hereby disclaims any responsibility for them.

Any people depicted in stock imagery provided by Getty Images are models, and such images are being used for illustrative purposes only. Certain stock imagery © Getty Images.

Scripture quotations are taken from the New King James Version. Copyright © 1982 by Thomas Nelson, Inc. Used by permission. All rights reserved.

ISBN: 978-1-6642-9223-9 (sc)
ISBN: 978-1-6642-9224-6 (hc)
ISBN: 978-1-6642-9222-2 (e)

Library of Congress Control Number: 2023902868

Print information available on the last page.

WestBow Press rev. date: 02/21/2023

To my wife of forty-five years, Jennie Whitt; my daughter, Amy Whitt Prickett, her husband, Jeremy, and their children, Emily and Tyler; and my son, Seth, his wife, Lanie Epps Whitt, and their children, Audra, Lizzy, and Perri.

Thanks to everyone who has blessed me in life and to those who encouraged me to write, especially to write a book.

Most of all, this book was written to honor the subject of these pages, Jesus Christ, my Lord, and Savior.

CONTENTS

PREFACE

The Awakening is the first book in the Journey of the Messiah series. This book was written in the first-person point of view, as if Jesus is speaking. It is written much like a memoir from Jesus, though the author is me. Please do not take this book as blasphemous. I do not consider this to be a "channeling of Jesus" or anything of the sort. It is only a unique perspective of my own, prayerfully inspired by my relationship with the Savior I serve, love, honor, and follow with all my heart.

This record is not from a dream or vision but from the rumblings of my spirit and mind. I do not consider this account to be free from error or ignorance. Within the framework of my own weaknesses, I have tried to be as truthful as possible as it relates to scripture. There is only one written account that I deem infallible, and it is the Bible, the Word of God. As much as I knew to do, I have adhered closely to the biblical accounts described within these pages.

There are many narratives contained within this book that are not found in the Bible, simply because those events are not recorded. These unrecorded events and conversations I have written about in the life of Jesus are from my own perspective and imagination. I am not attempting to write another Gospel.

If I have crossed any lines regarding the Bible, it is from my earthen vessel and not from the intent of my heart. The Journey of the Messiah series is my attempt to think how Jesus's journey on earth affected the Son of God, who was also the Son of Man. My hope is to open a window into which we can gaze and imagine.

I am a follower of Jesus and filled with the Spirit of God. In my life, I have tried to be a diligent student of the Bible and a casual student of history and cultures of the world. I began and continue this written Journey of the Messiah series as an adoring worshipper and devoted follower of Jesus. My prayer is that this writing will cause you to think and consider both those things written as well as things not said.

I believe in the deity of Jesus but also in the humanity of Jesus. He is all of God, in all of man. He is the second person of the Trinity. He is the Word made flesh.

My greatest desire is to bring light and glory to our Savior Jesus Christ and His uniqueness in all the universe and in all of eternity. Jesus Christ is the only Redeemer afforded to mankind. He alone gives salvation resulting in an abundant life on earth, and eternal life in heaven. I seek only to bring glory and honor to His name.

"And there are also many other things that Jesus did, which if they were written one by one, I suppose that even the world itself could not contain the books that would be written. Amen" (John 21:25 New King James Version).

Before we begin our Journey with the Messiah series in the pages of this book, *The Awakening*, please understand how I distinguished the names of deity and some of the characters. I have capitalized the first letter of all nouns and pronouns referring to all Persons of the Trinity: Father, Son, and Holy Spirit.

Also, so the reader will not be confused when Jesus is referring to His earthly parents and His Heavenly Father, the following words are used in this book:

- "Ima" is the word used by Jesus for His mother, Mary.

- "Abba" is the word used by Jesus for His stepfather, Joseph.
- "FATHER" is the word Jesus uses for His Heavenly Father.

Concerning the siblings of Jesus, he has four brothers named in the Bible—James, Joses (Joseph), Simon, and Judas (Jude)—and sisters who are not numbered or named (cf. Matt. 13:55–56). I have assigned names to three of these sisters: Maya, Elana, and Adina.

I pray you enjoy *The Awakening* that you hold in your hands. It came from my heart as an offering of honor to My Lord and hopefully a gift of inspiration and encouragement to those who walk in the dust of the earth.

CHAPTER ONE

TO THE CROSS, FROM THE CROSS

For He made Him who knew no sin to be sin for us, that we might become the righteousness of God in Him.

2 CORINTHIANS 5:21

From the beginning, I knew My life as the Son of Man would come to this torturous end. It was the redemptive plan of God for man, before man was to be. This knowledge did not make My pain any less but added grief to My agony. The weight of the sinful guilt for man is a knife to My soul as the nails are to My flesh. I hang between heaven and earth, bridging the gap for all time and for all who come by faith to drink My blood and eat My flesh.

The jeering crowd beneath Me is gawking at My demise on the cross. Through My clouded eyes, I can see the pierced heart of My mother as she witnesses the crucifixion of her firstborn, promised Son. Her emotional pain echoes the words of the old man Simeon, who prophesied on the occasion of her purification, forty days after My birth: "Behold, this Child is destined for the fall and rising of many in Israel, and for a sign which will be spoken against (yes, a sword will pierce through your own soul also), that the thoughts of many hearts may be revealed" (Luke 2:34–35).

The horror of the cross, invented from the depths of hellish hearts, was designed to maximize suffering in the victim and fear in the watchers. Glee from the executioners is the spatter from the boiling point of evil hearts.

My journey in flesh culminates with this harrowing end. This is not only the fulfillment of My walk among men but also the climax of FATHER's redemptive plan for man and creation. This is the taking of the sacred scroll from FATHER's hand and opening its seals.

My torture is magnified by the debt of humanity's sin and the wrath of My FATHER. Here on the cross, the grief of My mother on earth is dwarfed by the abandonment and wrath of My FATHER in heaven toward His Son. Though FATHER and I have always been one in absolute unison, now and for this moment We are conflicted and divided.

Even though I have been in perfect and sinless harmony with FATHER, the sins of the whole world and of all time are now imputed on My whole being. As I had been one with FATHER, now I am one with all the sinners of earth. Upon this cruel tree of judgment and condemnation, I bear the punishment for all the sin of fallen man. The retribution of death and destruction weigh totally upon Me.

The pain of My separation, for the reason of My imputed sin though I was sinless, is the anguish of My soul today. I feel the sore grief and helplessness of all the condemned who will stand before the white throne to be judged by God. It is necessary for Me to bear the unbearable sentence of those condemned to hell with "I never knew you; depart from Me!" (Matt. 7:23). The horror meant for those who were once known on earth but then were exiled, as if they had never been, into the oblivion and doom of hell, is Mine to bear upon the cross. For Me it will not be forever, but in this moment, it is as eternity.

I refused the Romans' cup of wine mixed with myrrh, but I willingly take FATHER's cup of wrath. I drink it all till no dregs remain. I take it all until nothing is left. The sword of God's vengeance for every murder, theft, and despicable sin of man pierces through My soul as the execution of all time. The world sees an execution of Rome, but I receive the execution from My loving FATHER as Judge and Avenger. The multiplied grief of My soul dwarfs the pain of My brutalized body.

The dreadful darkness in the noontime day is only a fraction of sin's darkness in My once spotless soul. I can feel the eternal annihilation of those who would be doomed to hell when the final gavel of judgment falls. My soul quakes like the earth on this dreadful day of My earthly ruin.

My shame and reproach are laid bare to the world, as My nakedness reveals. Gethsemane's seed of anguish is now bearing twice-rotten fruit on My body and in My heart. Unbearable—the word cannot describe what courses through Me. All the forces of being in Deity and creation seem pitted against My soul, bringing all creation to the brink of utter destruction. How did it come to this? The pure justice of God bringing mankind's full guilt of sin into complete account, weighed in the balance of My body and soul.

The unexplainable suffering of the cross is only articulated by the groans and screams of the punished men on this hill of torture called Golgotha, the place of the skull. My eternal purpose of becoming the sacrifice for man's sin does not lessen My anguish. The climax of judgment I bear comes into fullness until I can bear it no more. I scream out to Him who loves Me but has now turned away, blackening the sky: "My God, My God, why have You forsaken Me?" (Mark 15:33).

All had to come to this, but in the unmeasurable expanse of eternity, before I was the sacrifice for sin, I was Ima's son, and before I was her son, I AM.

CHAPTER TWO

BEFORE I WAS, I AM

·········~ⁿⁿ◦◊◦◊◦◊◦◊◦◊◦ⁿ◦◦~ⁿⁿ·········

In the beginning was the Word, and the Word
was with God, and the Word was God.

JOHN 1:1

I n the endless expanse of eternity, I Am, the Self-Existent One, exists as FATHER, Son, and Holy Spirit. We are One. Our magnificent glory envelopes Our unity of Deity in brilliant colors never dreamed by mortal men. Our unity is like a dance of unbroken rhythm and timing. It is like a dance of harmonious movement surrounded by colored wind wielding all wisdom and power. This is the dance I enjoyed forever: FATHER, Spirit, and I, the Son, dancing in unison as the One True God, of One Being yet distinct.

In Our dance, there are no missteps because We are One in perfection. We are the cadence of the expanse of all there is. We fill the vastness with Our joyful presence. The absolute union of Our wisdom and power is the nucleus of all that will be. The wonder known and experienced without any limitations is the boundlessness of Deity.

The gulf between earthly comprehension and eternal knowing

is a chasm that only We can span. One day I will leave this glorious state to walk in the limitations of a human existence. But for now, We dance in majestic splendor, in the joyful glory of all We are.

The mysteries of God are truths not yet revealed. The fragments of Our understanding revealed to men will be glorious and called prophesies and revelations. The greatness of Our Being cannot be written even in the mountainous volumes of men's scrolls. The parchment of men will contain only a jot of the reality of the whole of Our Being.

I Am is one of the many names by which We will reveal Ourselves. It is all encompassing, all knowing, and all powerful. There is nothing outside the realm of I Am that We are. The first human to hear this name will be the prophet Moses when We reveal Ourselves in the bush not consumed yet glowing as fire, just as Our created universe will emit an aura of Our glory but not be consumed. The glory of eternity is a supernatural spectrum permeated by Our very existence.

Having no equals and no rivals provides a peace that knows no threat. There will be enemies to Our dominance but no rivals, for We have no equal. They will be as dry straw to Our fiery flame of power. Our dance of eternity, in the brilliance of Our wisdom and strength, is saturated with indescribable peace and joy.

Lucifer, a once-anointed cherub, gathered a rebellion against Us, but the Adversary was soon banished with his rebel cohorts from the glorious sphere. The darkness that clouded his soul darkened the world to which We sent him. We knew this pompous cherub would come to this, and the orchestration of Our redemptive plan involved his future schemes. He would not be the last created vessel to come to dishonor.

Our power is such that a spoken word sends into instantaneous creation the reality of galaxies, worlds, and creatures. Such power can never be held in righteousness, except by the One who is fully inundated with love and wisdom. Power in the fallen world will easily corrupt into tyranny and oppression because it will not be held within the boundaries of love and wisdom. Our power is perfect; love, wisdom, and justice permeate it.

Moving in the cadence of eternity infused by love, power, and wisdom is the dance of God. It is the perfect movement of all there is, from the smallest atom to the largest galaxy. The twirling dance of God is the rhythm of the created world. The circular pattern of creation, from the electrons of atoms to the orbits of planets, reflect the divine dance of the Eternal One.

We are not dancing to an external rhythm; rather, the cadence of the universe is tuned to Our dance. We are the rhythm. All of time is held in Our moment; the entire span of eternity is unfolding in Our conscious present. Men's prophecies are only a few notes from Us to make known a hint of a revealed mystery.

And so, the rhythm of eternity continues with the dance of God. This was My existence as the Son of God before I came to be known as the Son of Man. I will be known on earth in the Hebrew tongue as Yehoshua and, in years to come, as Jesus the Christ, the Messiah.

My destiny was always known with Us. The consciousness of God is not understanding the known, but all that will be known comes forth from Us. With God there is no learning of what exists, but We set in motion all that will exist.

There was no beginning with Us as We are. Eternal existence knows no beginning or ending. As the Self-Existent One, there is no greater power, wisdom, or source of creation beyond Us. We are not the starting point because there is no designated point of beginning with Us. All that We are created all that will be. We have always been and will always be the I AM.

The concept of time is only a measure given to mark the segments of Our creation. We reign in eternity, as all of time is Our present. A thousand earth years in the past is not even a yesterday for Us. A thousand earth years in the future is not even a tomorrow to the Eternal One. The span of so-called time is not Our abode; it is only a musical scale for the notes of Our rhythm in the created universe.

We are the Eternal One, existing beyond the sphere of time with no past, present, or future. All of time is Our now. We do not merely remember the past and foresee the future. Our consciousness is in all of time and eternity.

In the record of Our Word given to mankind, the beginning of man's habitation is briefly described as, "In the beginning God created the heavens and the earth" (Genesis 1:1). Our eternal thread is woven into the fabric of time.

Here is the record of Our Creation. We first purposed to create a habitation for Our special created being called man. FATHER's wisdom encompassed the plan and uttered it out. When FATHER spoke, His breath, the Holy Spirit, moved from conception to execution and then to the Son's completion. FATHER spoke, Spirit executed, and I, the Son, completed the work of creation.

The banishment of Lucifer from Our glorious abode sent him to the earth, where man was to one day dwell. The destructive powers of Satan were put on full display as he marred the primordial beauty of creation to cold dark and chaotic waters that covered it. He took great joy in ruining all things with the fingerprint of God.

In the beginning, We created the heavens for glory and the earth for man's abode.

From the depth of FATHER's infinite wisdom, He exhaled His Word of creation. His breath would be known in the Hebrew tongue as *ruach*, translated "breath" or "spirit." FATHER's will and purpose, spoken forth from His eternal well of wisdom, was carried forth in power by Holy Spirit. I, the Son, completed the work, as I am also known as the Word, the finished breath.

We spoke light into being over the darkened and putrid waters. The first ray of light sent the darkness running for refuge. As wonderful as it was, this light was only a glimmer of Our infinite glory. Darkness now and in the future would hide from its brilliance and never find refuge.

The first day of Our Creation was a perfect wonder. We pronounced it good and continued Our creational celebration.

Then We spoke forth the atmosphere to separate the waters of the heavens from the waters of the earth. The miracle of Our suspension of water particles in the atmosphere was glorious. Our dance of circular pattern was seeded in the vapors of the earth, going from the atmosphere to earth and back again. Yes, it was good, and the second day was finished.

We birthed the land from the waters as the soil surged through the waves. Just as the rich ground rose from the waters, one day new life would come from wombs with a burst of water. The sheer joy of life abounds from the life of water. All of life would echo from water.

The bounds were surveyed so that the waters could go no further than their limits. As the land came from the waters, so the plants sprouted from the ground at Our Word. The bouquet of the flora of the earth abounded with mosses, grasses, bushes, and trees. The varieties were astounding and beautiful and would provide for the needs of the creatures to come.

In the plants, We provided propagation by roots, buds, stems, tubers, rhizomes, and seeds. The plants covered the earth with vibrant colors and shapes. We looked on as creative artists, and We all in unison said it was very good. It was the third day of Our Creation, and Our world was filled with light, moisture, land, and a multitude of plants.

We let the unhindered light reign over the third day so that the plants would have the full benefit of unlimited light. Then we organized the lights to distinguish the periods of darkness and light. The Sun star would rule the period of light called day. Its position in relation to the earth would set times and seasons, marking the passage of time and ships.

Next, We created the moon so its reflective light gave ambient light even at night. Its gravitational pull would set the tides of the earth's oceans. Men would chart time's monthly progression by its phases.

We also created the myriad of stars to add a sparkle to the night. They would be a roadmap for travelers and a wonder of discovery for the curious. The thought of men peering into the dark backdrop of night to connect the starry patterns brought Us immense joy. The fourth day was luminously good.

On the fifth day, We brought forth a multitude of birds to fly in the heavens and fish to fill the vast rivers, lakes, and oceans. In a moment, the skies filled with birds and the waters teemed with swimming creatures of all sorts. It was the fifth day of Our Creation, and it was good with fluttering birds of the air and swimming creatures of the waters.

On the sixth day of Our Creation, We brought land creatures from the substance of the earth. Our land creatures came forth from the same elements of the earth. Again, the creative dance brought forth a circular pattern conceived in the mind of God.

The dryland came alive with insects, reptiles, and mammals of abundance. The earth was filled with living creatures of every shape, size, color, and kind.

Earth was beautiful, vibrant, and good. Our creation was not for sheer beauty only; it was created for a purpose. We had created a habitation for the being likened unto Us. This wonderful creature would be the crowning glory of Our creative work.

None would be like him. Our intention was to give him and his offspring dominance over the created world.

We formed man from the dust of the earth. By Our hands, We sculpted him into a complete form, with a brain to search the depths of knowledge and truth. By Our wisdom, We designed his brain to reflect Our image of understanding. He would search the richness of creation, catalogue its varieties, and name its kind.

His hands were to have dexterity and skill, with the strength to fell a tree and the tenderness to hold a child. He would stand tall and walk upright as the regal creature of the earth.

His mouth would speak, sing, cry, and even whistle. The expression of his face had the capacity to communicate without saying a word. His eyes would see close enough to thread a needle and far enough to chart the heavens.

Man was formed from dust, and there he lay as cold as the soil. He was motionless for a moment. This majestic creature fully formed for function was lifeless and still. His current lifeless appearance would later become the look of a dead man.

From the reservoirs of Our wisdom came the essence of life. It filled the living of creation in the flora and fauna of the world. This essence is unmeasurable and can only be observed. The absence of it would be death; its presence would be astounding.

We leaned over the man of clay and gave a puff of Our lifegiving breath. Immediately, he gathered Our breath, and his form became a being, a living soul. We called him Adam. He breathed two breaths, sat up, and then stood. The first expression on his face was a smile as he basked in the flood of Our glory. He had an immediate understanding of who We were. After his first few breaths of inhaled life, he exhaled a word of worship. His first action upon the earth was pure and perfect worship of Us.

He was like Us in many ways. His composition was also a

triune being of a human spirit, a soulish nature, and a physical body. The creation of man was for eternity, but later he would become spiritually marred, bringing death to his natural body and brokenness to his spirit and soul. The corruption of his perfection would be passed to his descendants. But in the beginning of his existence, he was perfect.

We celebrated the form and life of Adam. He was everything We desired, lacking nothing. He bore Our image of an intelligent being capable of creation, caring, love, and understanding.

Adam immediately rushed into Our presence and delighted in Us with all jubilant wonder. This was the first moment of shared joy and ecstasy with a created being and his Creator. We encircled him in Our dance of Deity. He was fascinated by Our glory and, without thought, joined in perfect rhythmic dance as he twirled in Our midst. It was man's first dance of worship being in unison with Us.

The fellowship We had with Adam was complete. His worship of Us was flawless. This was the reason We had created man. He was the reason We had created this lush, verdant creation called earth.

We desired to bring all of mankind from this one created being. All people would come from one blood. In Adam was all who would ever be. He was the complete creation formed and brought forth by Us. Through him, all others would come into the world.

The next step in Our plan was to bring about another marvelous creature from the tissue of Adam. She would be his helpmate, taken from the nearness of his heart to walk beside him in all the endeavors of their dominion of the earth.

We put Adam into a deep sleep. Then We removed his rib and closed his flesh again. From the scion of his rib, We created the woman who would bring him even more completeness. She would be called Eve, the mother of all living beings. We took her from his side so that they would be inseparable in this perfect creation of Ours.

The graft for her substance was from near his heart and lungs. The heartbeat and the breath of life were the regions where the woman sprang from the man. He would become the spiritual head of the family, yet the woman would be the heart. It would take both in this beautiful pattern of unity to fulfill Our purpose in the family, on the earth.

His sleep was so sound, it took some time for Adam to wake. The completion of his healing took place while he slept.

When Eve took form and then life, she rose to her feet. She looked toward Us with a radiant smile of worship and adoration. Then she looked toward Adam. Her nurturing nature blossomed as We watched her compassion swell within her soul. Eve was drawn to Adam in his vulnerable state.

She knelt beside his slumbering body and embraced him. We absorbed the love radiating from her heart. Though this was the first touch of man and woman, it was as if they were eternal in their love.

While Adam slept, Eve cradled his head and moved her hands gently across his face. The tenderness of her hands and the radiance of her eyes showered the scene with the brilliance of perfect love. It was a glorious moment in the beginning of the journey of man and woman on earth.

When Adam opened his eyes from his induced sleep, he and Eve locked eyes for the first time. Their perfect love was immediate, with no hesitance. We had made them for each other, and they were perfect beings, making a perfect union.

Adam's image was mirrored in the image of the woman. He called her bone of his bones and flesh of his flesh. The bones represented the structure of the family, and flesh and blood represented the substance of life.

Their first day together would be a standard of love not matched after the fall of man. The absorption of their love for one another was not a lessening of their worship of Us; rather, it fulfilled their created purpose. They were one in Us, accomplishing the purpose of Our creation in perfect harmony, unadulterated purity, and enraptured joy. Future marital unions of men and women would initiate, and life would be conceived in this relation of love.

We instructed them to take dominion over the earth. They were the stewards over all creation. It would be their responsibility to fill the earth with their kind, to be fruitful and multiply.

We gave everything to them except one forbidden tree, the tree of the knowledge of good and evil. If they ate its fruit, death would be the result.

Satan in the form of the serpent beguiled the woman to sin. She ate of the fruit and gave to her husband. Sin entered, and man became spiritually marred and destined to die. Our righteous justice required death as the penalty for sin. The dominion over creation had been forfeited by man's disobedience; thus, creation fell under the sway of Satan's destructive forces.

We had to banish the created couple from the garden, and so, death entered the creation through man. Adam and Eve would live long lives on the earth, but eventually the penalty of death would come due.

We of the Triune knew the Son of God would need to be born into Our created world through the flesh of mankind. Our unbreakable justice required the penalty of death. The final and complete eternal penalty for sin would be in the plan of the ages when I, the Son of God, became the Son of Man. Coming as a man, I would bring redemption over sin and death by My sacrificial death and victorious resurrection of life.

CHAPTER THREE

IT IS TIME

The Holy Spirit will come upon you, and the power of the
Highest will overshadow you; therefore, also, that Holy
One who is to be born will be called the Son of God.

LUKE 1:35

We had created the world together and watched Our plan unfold upon the earth. In his futile mind, man had thought he controlled his own destiny and made his own way. We watched the ploys of men, even the evil ones, play into Our orchestration of events.

Our purpose and man's time were intricately woven together into Our plan on the earth. The events of man's history, as harsh as some were, fell into the arrangements for Our destiny.

It was what We knew from the forever, but the journey of man through time must be completed to this point. FATHER's timing is always perfect, and now was the time. Prophesies of My coming had been given to man so they would expect Me, hope for My coming, and perhaps receive a hint of who I AM.

At the appointed time, I was to leave Our heavenly dance in the eternal state to walk as a man on the earth. We were excited that the time was ripe for the fulfillment of the ages, yet I was sad to leave the fullness of joy for the brokenness of Earth. This was the first great sacrifice of the Son of God, and it was destined and known from the beginning.

I knew Holy Spirit would escort Me with the transition from heaven to earth. We knew what this entailed, but now it was time for the execution of salvation upon a broken world. My arrival would be without fanfare and barely noticed by a puzzled few. The audience of heaven was at full attention for the moment of fulfillment.

We knew that in a mere moment, I would be translated from eternal glory to the conception level of human flesh. I would be in a dormant self-existent haze for a few of man's years. At a moment in My human life, I would awaken to My reality. Later, I would be rejoined by Holy Spirit in the spiritual dimension as He empowered mortal men.

I was one with FATHER and Spirit, but now My journey as a man made it necessary for a change in dynamics. My existence in the eternal state was only as God, but now I was to dwell in the being of a man. I would be empowered by FATHER and later by Holy Spirit.

It would be necessary for Me to live within the limitations of a human body and mind. Before My incarnation, I was the ever-present Son of God, but as the Son of Man, I could only be at one place at any given time. I was the all-knowing Son of God, but as the Son of Man, I had to learn as any child of flesh learned. I was the all-powerful Son of God, but as the Son of Man, I had to rest and sleep, as My body would tire. On the day of My passion, My body—beaten and weak—would need the assistance of a humble man, Simon of Cyrene, to bear the wood of My execution.

My journey would be the same as mankind's in many ways but also very different. My inner spirit was not marred as their spirit. All men are born *of* flesh; I would be born *in* flesh. Men have an innate enmity with My Holy FATHER, yet I had an eternal and holy connection with Him. They have a propensity for sin, but My nature was one of righteousness. My birth via the virgin would affirm My conception by God.

Once rejoined by Holy Spirit at My baptism in the waters of the Jordan, I would be empowered in the same pattern afforded to men. My life would not only be for the purpose of redemption but also the manifestation of mankind's potential when empowered by Holy Spirit. Only one man would live sinless: Me.

At the time of My departure from Heaven, FATHER said the time was upon Us. Suddenly, it seemed like the angelic host quieted to a holy hush. Never since the creation and assignment of the angels in the eternal bliss had it seemed possible for even a momentary separation of the Son from FATHER and Spirit. Now Spirit and I were positioned at the portal for My transfer to the virgin and to the world.

For the angelic host of God, trust is never in question, yet understanding is sometimes lacking. They only knew to trust. The warring angels raised their swords in a unison salute. The ministering angels bowed in reverence, uttering a harmonious angelic chant.

The plan of salvation for the world had been in motion, but now the fulfillment was to be executed by My entrance into the sphere of men.

In the heart of FATHER was an overwhelming love for man. From Adam's first breath, We simply adored him. He was made in Our image. We loved to watch his mind work to create solutions to simple problems. His first creation was a small basket, woven from small branches of a tree, that he used it to carry fruit.

In his heart was a great love for the creatures around him, reminiscent of Our love for him and Eve. He played with the tiger cubs as they scampered through the garden and played tag with the young monkeys. Much like an artist admiring his painting or a composer listening to her music, We loved to watch Our creation.

The first family of earth was a fulfillment of Our creative plan. Adam and Eve were harmonious and unified in the very likeness of the heavenly union of FATHER, Son, and Spirit. The tenderness, admiration, and love with which they touched one another sent a wave of fulfillment through the winds of Our Spirit.

When they succumbed to the deceit and temptation of the enemy, We were grieved more than all the burials that would follow their kind's demise. They would grieve and cry at the burial of their son Abel and the banishment of their son Cain. When they sinned, We grieved the pain and tears of the multitude of deaths that would follow their downfall.

When Adam was created perfect and complete, We knew his excellence would be corrupted by sin and result in death. His fall would overcome his life and all he would sire. The Beloved Apostle will describe Me as the "Lamb slain from the foundation of the world." (Rev. 13:8). This was always in Our purpose, to redeem Our own creation by My coming as a creature. My death would fulfill Our own justice and principles of eternal righteousness. Man sinned; man must pay the debt. I, the Son of Man, was the man Redeemer from before time, who was also God.

Now standing at the portal, I was poised not only between heaven and earth but also life and death. The lower creation had become as before, filled with darkness and chaos. Just as in the scrolls of creation, Holy Spirit would hover over the darkness and lifelessness, bringing light and life into the brokenness of man's story. Man's story of fallenness was to become My story of redemption.

This moment, and the months that followed in man's history, would be recorded as glorious, but in heaven the mood was heavy. The angelic multitude closed into a tighter circle of anticipation. My sacrifice would begin as I departed the glories of heaven for the trials of earth. Heaven and earth would never be the same.

Father simply said it was time. When the breath of His Word was released, Holy Spirit and I rapturously exited the portal of heaven. Within that moment, I knew I would succumb to the dormant state of embryonic consciousness. There was no lapse of time but an eternal velocity of instantaneous implantation of My spirit in My earthly mother's womb.

I foreknew from this conception that this would be My journey. I would be in a self-induced dormancy from eternal awareness until the time of My messianic awareness.

As the Self-Existent One, I foreknew what would happen, but My actual experience had to be that of a man. Even though I was equal with God, it was necessary to humble Myself as a man. The sacrifice for man's sin could only be by man's blood, but all before Me were tainted souls. Father said it, and I knew I would be the Son of Redemption to redeem a lost humanity when I assumed the role of man to redeem what man had corrupted and lost.

I knew Holy Spirit would translate Me from Our glorious habitation to the womb of a young village girl named Mary. Ima was the name I would call her in the language of our people. I had witnessed from heaven as Gabriel spoke to her. She was so bewildered by the message but was receptive in her humility to bear what Father deemed for her to be and to do.

The man she was betrothed to was Joseph, whom I would call Abba. He was a builder and carpenter by trade. He had labored hard so that he could sustain his future wife and family. Joseph was eager, as most young men were, to have a wife, children, and a home. This was the aim of the people of the world.

The people of God had lived under the tyrannical Roman Empire. Taxes were high, and most had to scrape out a living with their backs and hands. It was not an easy life, but the populace tried to do as they could to make a contented life amid their dire circumstances.

FATHER, in His wisdom, had designed the family to be the building block of society. He had put this into the heart of man to gather as a family, then as a clan, then as a tribe, and then as a nation. We had ordained and called Abraham the father of Our people. Then Moses was the prophet called to lead Our people out of Egyptian bondage and into the land of promise.

Centuries had rolled by as My people had gone from worship to idolatry and back again. The Law was written on a scroll, but the time was coming when My words would be written on their hearts. A new paradigm of worship was to come. My people's history was a history of struggle. I was coming to call them to rest in God and to worship in spirit and truth.

My mother-to-be was a simple girl who heard a difficult message, yet she surrendered to the message of Gabriel. The mark of My special ones was not in their own strength but in their surrender and obedience to My call. It was not necessary for her to completely understand the message; however, it was necessary for her to completely surrender to it.

I felt the inner struggle of her soul as she bore the Righteous One while also bearing the shame of a sinner. Oh the irony of this world I would invade. My mother, a humble village girl, in the innocence of her virginity would bear the Redeemer from sin while enduring the scorn and ridicule that came with accusations of being an adulterous, sinful woman.

The orchestration of events on the earth are often hidden by clouded eyes of those who should know. We turn the hearts of kings as We wish. Caesar Augustus, the Roman emperor, had called for a new tax. The people of his occupied territory of Israel were ordered to return to their ancestral cities so that a proper census could be counted.

Since My mother-to-be was espoused to Joseph, who was of the House of David in Bethlehem, it was necessary for them to travel to Bethlehem. This alignment of events had to come about for the fulfillment of scripture, because the Messiah was the Son of David from Bethlehem.

Gabriel told her that she was highly favored, but this did not exempt her from the troubles of earth. Her difficulties of dealing with an untimely pregnancy would result in My timely delivery in Bethlehem.

I knew Ima's burden would be a parallel of My journey in this broken world. Just as she would bear the shame of uncommitted sin for the purpose of God; as the Righteous One, I would die as a slandered sinner to redeem a corrupt world. Not only would I bear their sin but also their shame.

In her womb, I began as any other child, but not as any other man because she was a virgin. My conception was not with human sperm but by the Spirit of God. The ovarian egg from Mary was fertilized by the same lifegiving Spirit of God whose breath filled the lungs of the first man of dust.

This beginning of life in the woman was My beginning as the Son of Man, and I would grow as every human conceived. Spirit hovered over her just as He hovered over the waters in the dark world. I became life in her, and I was the Son of Man. I had existed from eternity never beginning, but I was now beginning anew as a conceived Son of Man.

This was a new dynamic for Us. The environment of the eternal abode had never had the absence of the Son. I was now in a state of fetal dormancy in the womb of a virgin, a village girl, awaiting the three decades of man's years before showing Myself to the world.

The patience and purpose of God is revealed in My coming, because a thousand years is as one day with Us. Being the Self-Existent One in eternity counters the different perspective of man's short years. I had to humble Myself to the constraints of a human existence to carry out the plan of FATHER.

My consciousness in the womb and in the early time of babyhood were just as any other child. I had no memory of being born, of the shepherds' visit, of the first suckle on My mother's breast, or even of My circumcision at eight days old.

Some of My first memories were as a toddler. I remember Ima holding Me close and singing as she looked into My eyes. She sang a psalm about FATHER and His everlasting mercy and His love so deep. The melody of her voice soothed Me, and the words had an unusual sound of familiarity, like a poet listening to his own poem being read in a voice other than his own.

I felt so secure in her arms in this insecure world. Little by little, I learned to be a part of a different existence. I was so loved by Ima; she was My mother, and I was her child. Our hearts were knit together with the bond My FATHER had designed for a child and his mother. It was a bond of mutual love. My young heart yearned for her love, and My life was soothed by her touch and words. No one on earth could cause Me to rest and be at peace as My loving mother could.

FATHER truly said she was highly favored. The love in her eyes spoke volumes without a word. Her touch was so gentle, My infant soul was captivated by her presence. She was gentle but also strong, making My infant emotions feel secure. The sound of her voice to My young ears reminded Me of a distant sound, now vague but it would be louder as I grew—the comforting voice of the Spirit of God.

As I grew, she made Me soft food with blended goat's milk and watched over Me like a hen over her chick. I noticed her looking at Me in a loving but strange way, as if she were trying to read My destiny in My eyes. I recall the hours of her holding Me close, looking into My face with nothing but adoration and love.

I had a mother, but I also had an earthly father. Abba was chosen for Me as much as Ima. I recall scenes in My memory of Abba carrying Me aloft on his shoulders. Whereas Ima had the soft touch of a gentle mother, Abba gave Me another level of strength and security. Even as a child, I could sense the strength he instilled in our family.

Many lessons of childhood would be woven into My preaching many years later. The house built on a firm foundation was carried from the many times Abba laid a foundation of stone for a home. The parable of the soils would reflect My grandfather sowing a small patch of lentils. And the woman mixing the leaven in three measures of meal was none other than Ima doing the same.

When I needed comfort, I ran to Ima. The times I needed strength, I turned to Abba. FATHER had designed the family as a balance of nurture and strength. In Our wisdom, We designed it, and in My humanity, I was able to live and thrive in it.

Ima held Me close in My childhood and released Me into the hands of God in My adulthood. As the old prophet would declare, a sword would pierce her gentle heart as she viewed the sacrifice of the ages.

CHAPTER FOUR

VILLAGE BOY

*And the Child grew and became strong in spirit, filled
with wisdom; and the grace of God was upon Him.*

LUKE 2:40

We—FATHER, Son, and Spirit—knew that My journey to earth as a man would require My life to be much like all other men. I had to learn as most children learned.

From the eternal side of My incarnation, I knew every minute of My young life-to-be in flesh. I knew every aspect of My conception, birth, infant life, early toddler years, and the entirety of My life on earth. However, I also knew that upon My incarnation, much of My omniscience would be clouded by My humanity. It would be meted out by FATHER as needed. How could a finite human brain hold the vastness of God's wisdom, knowledge, and understanding?

As I became older, I had the same vagueness of childhood memories as most men. I did not remember My first step or the first time I drank from a cup with My own hands.

I remembered a few moments in My early years as if they

were a dream but knew them to be real. We were gathered as a family and Abba was praying to FATHER. I was in My fourth year of life on earth. As he prayed, My spirit was stirred as if an overflowing fluid would burst from My soul. Ima was holding Me, and she noticed My little body shaking mildly. Not knowing what was happening, she pulled Me close to her bosom to comfort Me. I did not need to be comforted, because I sensed a deep, resounding peace and a call from beyond our little village home. My body was held securely in Ima's lap, but My spirit longed to soar heavenward along with the heart cry of My Abba, who was praying to My FATHER.

I remember that the waves of emotions took some time to subside while Ima stroked My head and tried to sooth Me with her motherly comfort. It was one of those touching moments of early childhood that lingered through the years. Ima remembered it as well, and later in life related to Me her feeling at the time. She had known who I was, but it and other happenings like it had shocked her back to the reality of who she held in her arms.

I did not have childhood memories of My brother James's birth, but I had shards of memories of Joses as an infant. My young memories of My younger brothers and sisters' births were vivid and plain.

Some of My first responsibilities were to watch My siblings for short periods of time until Ima retrieved something from a near neighbor's home. Even though I was the oldest, Ima had an inherent trust in Me that slightly irritated My brothers nearest My age.

James, My oldest brother, and Jude, the youngest brother, had serious sides to their personalities, but they could also be quite adventurous. The two middle brothers, Joses and Simon, were carefree pranksters. We all scuffled in play, and the four would try to multiply their efforts to overcome Me. Often I would let them win and play it up that they were so strong.

My darling little sisters—Maya, Elana, and Adina—were quite another story. They treated Me like a junior father since I was careful to keep them from harm. When Ima left them in My care, I watched over them like a shepherd caring for his sheep. I was very protective of them, and they enjoyed My careful attention.

My sisters were fun-loving but gracious in every way. As much as My brothers could be brash, My sisters were the very opposite in their kind and considerate ways. Maya was a little more serious than the younger two. They could be a little lazy with their chores, and Ima scolded them for not staying on task. It was humorous how their dishwashing chores could easily change into a splash bath. They were such fun-loving girls.

They knew of My deep love for them, and they reflected the admiration back to Me. They loved to comb My hair with a big comb Abba had whittled from a cow horn flattened by heat. I feigned pain with their combing, and they would break into a big wave of giggles. Oh My little sisters!

I knew James and Joses loved Me and respected My position as oldest brother to a degree. They were not rebellious by nature, but being the two nearest My age, they had to try Me from time to time just to show their masculinity. I learned to make My idea their idea. They did not take to bossing too well, so I had to make My intentions more presentable. I began to realize that life in a functioning family was the training ground for life in the grown-up world. These moments of understanding came as My wisdom of life increased. Once I learned these principles of life, it was strangely as if I had always known them.

I was more protective of My sisters, for I knew they would always have a brother, father, or husband to protect them in our society. My brothers, on the other hand, had to learn to fend for themselves and their families. It was more important in our culture for My brothers to know how to live in this harsh and sometimes cruel world.

In the future, during the early time of My ministry, My brothers would be doubtful of who I was. It would take time and events before they would see Me as more than their brother. I was always patient with them, never dismissive. It was necessary for them to come not to a point of understanding but to a point of faith in their ultimate relationship with Me. They would need to believe in Me, not just see Me as an older brother who preached.

When I was old enough to wander the village beyond the watchful eyes of My parents, I played with My friends in the village. I also fetched water from the well and ran errands for Abba. The unhurried life of the village was set on the local harvest and the festivals of the Jews. Our lives were routine but on the edge, just above survival. My people rarely dreamed of anything beyond their present reality of food, water, and shelter.

We never hungered, but the supply of grain was never bountiful. Ima watched our supply like a hawk. She was careful to store our grain in an earthen vessel with a wooden lid to keep out the hungry rats looking for a morsel. We foraged the hillsides for wild herbs and edible plants. Ima used the combinations of herbs, native greens, spices, and salt to flavor the oil used for dipping our bread. Ima was diligent to instruct her children about the edibles we foraged from the land.

Lentil stew with flatbread was a regular meal on our table. Meat was rare, and it was usually present on certain days of feasting with our religious holy days. Eggs and cheese were other foods that broke the monotony of bread and sauce. We sun-dried fruit in the hot sun to help spread the bounty over months of scarcity. We usually ate fruit and vegetables while they were in season. Occasionally, we had fresh fish. Sometimes Ima bought salted and dried fish from the local market. She sometimes used the dried fish as an ingredient in other dishes.

Work and survival were all My people had known in their lives. The usual complaints were of the weather, poor crops, or evil treatment by the Romans. Everyone in our village was thankful to have food for the day and live into their sixty years of life by God's mercy. Expectations beyond that were only for the dreamers of our people.

I grew in knowledge and wisdom as I grew in stature. My perspective of life began to grow and to change. My family mentioned My point of view was quite different than others'. My acute awareness of people and life was beyond the other boys in the village. They seemed to live in the moment without any introspection or broader perception of life.

I noticed My understanding about weighty matters such as life, death, and spiritual questions were like older men who had lived many more decades than Me. I would lay on My mat at night and think through the events of the day, down to the minute details of interactions with and observations of people. It was like I could see into their eyes and go deeper into their souls than they would have been comfortable knowing.

One day, Ima and I visited a near neighbor, Asa, who was sick. Ima carried a pot of delicious lentil stew and some flatbread she had prepared. Our visit was mostly to deliver the food and to express a kind word of concern.

Ima called from the closed gate and was immediately invited in by Samara, whose husband was sick. Ima set the pot of stew on a rug and motioned for Me to put the basket of flatbread next to it. Ima and Samara chatted, and I wandered over to the mat where Asa lay. I asked him how he was doing. He cracked his eyes open and answered, "I am not well, son," as he closed his eyes again.

Ima saw Me out of the corner of her eye and immediately told Me not to disturb Asa.

He replied, "He's not adding to my suffering."

His words struck Me as strange. I was not adding to his suffering, meaning I was not bothering him. His words jolted My heart. No, I was not adding to his suffering; neither was I taking any away. Compassion suddenly arose in My heart for him, and I yearned to take away his suffering. Deep within, I could sense his physical pain, weariness of soul, and fear of leaving his family without support.

Ima and Samara joined Me by his side. Sensing the presence of the two women, Asa opened his eyes again. Ima asked him how he was doing today. He replied that he was no worse but no better. She asked if the local physician had visited and given any ointments. Samara said they had put a poultice on his chest that smelled like dried fish mixed with sour wine.

He gave a weary smile. "The poultice smelled like death." He tried to laugh, but it only threw him into a fit of coughing. Then there was a moment of silence.

I blurted out, "Have you prayed?"

Ima looked at Me, startled, not believing My bold question. Samara looked a little embarrassed, as if that had not been their first thought. Asa gave a soft, subdued chuckle at such a question from a young village boy.

Countering My insistent question, he said, "You pray!"

Asa thought his statement would challenge My question, and I would find My proper place in his house. I looked at Ima for permission before doing or saying anything else. Not knowing what to do in this awkward moment, she sheepishly nodded her approval.

I did not seek Asa's approval. I simply began to pray. "Adonai, Maker of heaven and earth. You have created all things and filled the world with Your life. We praise You for Your great power and might. We thank You for the bread of this day and Your life in our bodies. We graciously ask You to rid Asa of this sickness and that Your life-giving power bring wellness again to his body. You are the great I Aм! Amen."

Asa looked up at Me with one eye open in a squint. "Well, that was quite a prayer for a boy. Son, thank You for Your concern and prayer. Perhaps, Adonai will hear Your prayer." With that, he closed his eyes and fell silent.

At this, Ima motioned for Me to follow her home. We left with no more words spoken. I could see Ima was disturbed but not at Me. She looked more bewildered, like someone taken off guard by a remark. Upon arriving home, she went about her business of cleaning dishes. I went outside to sit and think.

She said nothing more about it as we finished our day. When the last child was situated on his mat and the lamp was blown dark, I whispered a prayer under My breath and closed My eyes to needed sleep.

The next thing I knew, it was morning. The morning sun threw amber rays across the eastern sky. One by one, we begin to scurry about our mornings. Today's breakfast meal was a boiled egg and bread from yesterday's hearth.

My morning chore, with My little sisters in tow, was to fetch water from the village well. We pulled the well cover and filled our earthen vessels with water. I carried the largest vessel and gave each of My little sisters a smaller jug, which they hoisted to their shoulders and balanced with one hand. I smiled as they went waddling back home with their jugs of water, looking the very image of miniature village women. They were in training for the chore of their lives, even though they were unaware. Drawing water at the well in the cool of the morning and carrying it home would be a daily routine for the remainder of their lives.

Passing Asa's house, we saw him slowly walking through the door, supported at his elbow by his wife. He smiled and in a weakened voice said, "Young man, you pray well. Look, the sick man is walking today!"

I simply smiled and said, "Praise Adonai!"

Samara motioned with hands, silently indicating, *See, he's walking.* Then she echoed My words, "Praise Adonai."

Hours later, Ima came from the outside and said to me, "Did you see Asa this morning? He is much better."

"Yes, Ima," I answered. "I saw him when we returned from the well. I am thankful to see he is much better, and we will pray for complete wholeness, yes?"

"Oh yes, my son, we shall," she answered, smiling.

With the passing of days, we could see Asa improving. In times past, Asa and Samara had only regarded Me as Mary's son or as any other village boy, but now they took a greater interest. They would smile and call Me by name instead of "son" or "boy."

I thought it strange that My people, who worshipped FATHER, would think it odd or unusual when He answered our prayers. I had no doubt and was confused by theirs.

We were happy to see Asa fully recovered. One day, he called Me over to his home. He expressed his thankfulness for My prayer. Asa told Me he had surrendered himself to die, for the disease had wearied him of life. His hope had drained from his soul like his physical strength from his body.

I knew this was the plight of the sick of the earth. It was more than physical disease but oppression of the soul as well. The sinful and dying state of this world would not only bring about sickness of body but also wearisomeness of soul.

Sometime after Asa had fully recovered, Samara came for a visit. She and Ima were close neighbors and friends. They were distant kin as well. I was doing a chore when Ima called Me over and into their conversation.

Samara spoke up with no introduction. "Jesus, I need to tell you something. When Asa was sick, we knew he was dying. Our eyes had seen the same sickness take away many friends. We were scared and worried. As we all do, we tried to keep hope alive by our words, but our hearts were melted with fear. I was counting the days before I would be a helpless widow and My children fatherless.

"The day You and Your mother visited, when You prayed, we were ashamed. We had not thought to pray to Adonai for healing. Also at the time, we thought Your question was one spoken by an ignorant little boy who did not understand. Asa told Me that he was a little offended at the time. So he countered Your question with a challenge to pray. Surprisingly, You prayed instead of feeling shame. But now we know You were right.

"We both know without any doubt that God answered Your prayer. I wanted to say thank You for believing and for Your powerful prayer. Thank You!"

I looked at Ima. Tears flowed down her olive cheeks.

"I am thankful to Adonai for healing Asa," I replied. Then I added, "I am thankful you still have your husband and can continue to be a wife and not a widow."

"Oh, Mary, such a wise son you have!" she told Ima.

I smiled and excused Myself to finish My household job. Minutes later, I heard Samara leave for her home.

Ima came in, looked at Me without saying a word, and then embraced Me tight in her arms. I could feel her sobbing. She released Me as if to say something profound but only silence remained.

I broke the awkwardness saying, "Praise Adonai!"

"Oh yes," she said. "Praise Adonai!"

Nothing more was mentioned in our household about Asa's healing. For the next few weeks, I could see people in the village looking at Me and whispering to each other. Asa and Samara had told their story of healing from household to household. The stares and whispering ceased in a month, and I assumed My usual place in the village.

Other villagers became sick, and some died. No one called for Me to pray for the sick; neither did I did feel compelled to pray as with Asa. I still believed and knew that something was growing inside My heart. The flower had budded but not bloomed.

Often when the elders gathered under the shade of a tree, their talk was about our people's situation with the Roman occupation. Inevitably, this type of talk led to the subject of the Messiah. Most had an idea of when He would come, what He would do, or who He would be. Much of the speculation was based on desperation, wishful thinking, or hearsay.

They had a vague belief of eventual deliverance of Israel from the oppression of the Romans. A messianic-like kingdom restored as in the days of David and Solomon was their elevated hope. Even their most misguided concept of the Messiah, at the very least, gave them a flicker of hope in the difficulties of their present days.

Our people's history was retold by our elders, especially in the synagogues. People spoke about our reliance on Adonai, but to most it was a far-fetched reality cloaked in the religious talk of men. We prayed, sang, and celebrated our festivals, but the people were veiled from a true worship grounded in spirit and truth.

My spirit was pure, yet the environment around Me was corrupted by sin. Even My wonderful parents were flawed by the fallenness around them and in them. Those less constrained by ritual and religion were even more susceptible to the failures of flesh. The Law of our people set boundaries for sin to a degree as a guard over the gates of their lives.

Once in the village, I was watching older boys playing with sticks as if they were swords. One of the boys became furious when he was wacked on the head by another boy. I could see the rage in his eyes, and I knew the rage came from deep within him. It was a strange thing for Me because I did not understand the hate he showed. It was as if he had a well of bitter water within his soul from which I had never drunk. When My messianic awareness came, I remembered the boy and knew his spirit was broken as all men's spirits are broken.

As I grew old enough to help without getting in the way, Abba gave Me tasks with the carpenter work. At first, I gathered small scraps of wood and carried them to My mother for the fire she used to cook our meals. Abba began to teach Me simple things of his trade as I grew into adolescence.

I resembled My mother. My nose, cheekbones, and chin looked like hers. People often commented about My eyes. Although they were dark like most, they said they were bright and perspective. Ima said I was an insightful child. At first, I did not know what that meant. However, I began to see that something inside Me was different from others. When FATHER answered My prayer to heal Asa, it had brought a new level of realization to Me. The faith in Me was strong, yet most people's expectation of God was doubt-ridden. In early boyhood, the sense of My messianic awareness was vague, but the journey toward it began to grow.

CHAPTER FIVE

THE AWARENESS

⸺⸻ ·⸱⸲⸳∞⟡⟐⟐⟐⟡∞⸲⸱· ⸻⸺

You are the Christ, the Son of the living God.
MATTHEW 16:16

M y parents were faithful Jews. We went to synagogue
every Sabbath and to Jerusalem on the required feast
days. Every morning and evening, we as a family
repeated the *Shema*. Abba would gather us together and lead us in
the Jewish prayer.

"Hear, O Israel: The LORD our God, the LORD is one! You
shall love the LORD your God with all your heart, with all
your soul, and with all your strength. And these words which I
command you today shall be in your heart. You shall teach them
diligently to your children, and shall talk of them when you sit in
your house, when you walk by the way, when you lie down, and
when you rise up. You shall bind them as a sign on your hand, and
they shall be as frontlets between your eyes. You shall write them
on the doorposts of your house and on your gates" (Deut. 6:4–9).

When we repeated the *Shema*, My heart would soar, and I
would go to a place in My heart that was glorious yet dreamlike.
There was something in My spirit that was calling Me from

beyond My present habitation. I was reaching for something that was just beyond My grasp, but I knew one day I would hold it.

Since I was a young boy of five years old, I had attended school at the synagogue, where the teaching was primarily the memorization of the Torah and the oral traditions. I had learned much of the scripture with the teaching of our leader of the synagogue.

As I approached twelve years old, the dreamy inner sense of who I was began to unroll as a scroll, fully manifesting itself into My messianic awareness.

It was not that I discovered the messianic awareness but rather that the awareness discovered Me. The stirring in My heart grew until one day, I came to the full understanding of who I was. Scenes from My eternal past began to crease through My brain, accompanied by an indescribable peace and joy. The scenes of the past were not of My childhood in Nazareth or in Ima's arms but of before My earthly conception. I heard FATHER's voice, and I caught glimpses of glory in My mind's eye. At first it was like bits and pieces of a dream, yet it was more reality than My present existence.

As My messianic awareness began to be revealed, I realized I was a stranger in a different world. This was the world I had grown up in as a child. I had a mother and a father, along with brothers and sisters, but I knew there was a connection beyond Nazareth in the world unseen by human eyes.

I was comfortable in the routine of My life. The work in the family household was often exhausting but also refreshing and purposeful. The joy of the family dynamic was life-giving. All the children in our family felt the love of Abba and Ima, and it was nourishment to our young souls. My relationship with My siblings was a constant dynamic of controlled chaos filled with joy.

The comfort level in My family structure was secure and

strong, but the longing of My spirit was beyond our little abode. I was drawn heavenward while My feet were firmly planted on the ground.

When the first glimmers of the messianic awareness began to invade My young life, I became less fulfilled by the usual prayers in the synagogue or during our daily family prayers. I savored the moments of our spiritual life at home and in the synagogue, but there was a gnawing of something much more.

There was an indescribable urge to get alone, to go behind the veil of this world. Often I hurriedly finished My chores and, to find an escape from My curious siblings, hiked up the deserted hill to a clump of rocks and shrubs. I found My spot and began to talk to FATHER in heaven. This excursion of prayer continued for months. Each time I could sense an upward intensification in My spiritual life.

As always, My prayers were fervent and fulfilling, yet the more I prayed, the more I could feel the presence of FATHER. I was setting the pattern for My spiritual life on earth, but I was also setting a pattern for those seeking to reach new depths of communion with God. This was the pattern I began. It was not a forced ritual of religion but rather like a deep drink of refreshing water on a hot day.

My life of prayerful communion with FATHER continued to grow and develop. I could sense in My spirit the gathering of pregnant clouds filled with drops of glory that would eventually flood My soul. At first, it was like a great expectation in My spirit without knowing the full weight of its fulfillment.

One day, I climbed the little dusty trail to My place of prayer. I found My spot and turned My face heavenward to the white puffy clouds positioned in the forefront of a beautiful blue sky. It was a beautiful day. There was a light breeze blowing from the southwest that cooled My sweaty face. Settling in for prayer, I felt the presence of FATHER as if I were about to soar to the white clouds over My head.

I bowed on My knees to call to FATHER from the depths of My heart. My spirit began to rise with each influx of glory waves. I was in a familiar place of prayer but strangely in a new mode of worship. In My twelve years of life on earth, there had been whiffs of another world. I knew there was something beyond this shrouded world. In My young life, I'd had dreams and fragmented moments from another sphere.

Immediately as I found My words, I could feel FATHER's powerful presence even greater. I had known My family's love and even the embrace of FATHER in prayer, but this was so vastly different. This love was so intense and pure, enveloping Me in such a strong caress that I never wanted to leave this moment. My earthly time quickly transfigured to the timeless flow of eternity.

I was in a spiritual daze as the layers of this world began to peel away, and I felt enraptured by the realm of eternity. My spirit soared to another known domain, and I was suspended in eternity even though My feet were on clay. I no longer sensed the wind on My face but felt the *Breath of God*.

Then, just as wave after wave of the sea crash against the shoreline, I felt swells of peace. It was the peace that could end every war and unite the worst of enemies. It was a peace beyond sheer joy, yet it brought tears to My eyes. This joyful peace flooded My young soul, and My inner spirit was twirling in a dance once so eternally familiar but now almost new.

FATHER and Spirit suspended My soul in a cloud that was encompassed in eternity. My inner spirit overwhelmed My earthly being. My spirit danced in perfect harmony and rhythm with FATHER and Spirit. Here on this dusty hilltop of Nazareth, I was one with the eternal twirling dance of Deity. Time on earth was no more, and eternity flowed seamlessly. I was one with the One. The unison dance of the Self-Existent One twirled in the spiritual realm with earth out of view. The glorious cloud of wisdom, power, and peace encapsulated Me in a membrane of joy. I could even smell the wonderful fragrance of heaven's bouquet of blossoms.

Then the joy waves hit Me so deep that I burst into laughter. The ruler in our synagogue surely would have scolded My exuberance, but I felt no hint of guilt. My emotions overflowed with wondrous fullness until I cried and then laughed. Then I laughed until I cried again. I found Myself going from kneeling to lying on My back facing the sky. I knew the ground to be hard, but the elation of My soul caused the sensation to be as if I was lying in My FATHER's warm embrace on a pillow of glory.

Then I sighed into deep quietness. Enveloped in this deep presence with FATHER, I lay contemplating this experience that quickened in Me of an earlier forever moment of glory and peace. It was glorious in My spirit, though overwhelming for My human mind, to comprehend all that had just happened.

It had been more than just a spiritual or even emotional experience, but it had also been an impartation of understanding. In these moments of eternal suspension, FATHER had revealed in the depth of My spirit the reality of who I was. I knew with full knowledge and no doubt that I was the Son of God, the Messiah. It was an illuminating realization of God being My FATHER and of My conception in My mother while she was an innocent virgin. While in this mist of eternity, FATHER had allowed Me to experience the eternal connection before My earthly time.

It was much for even a twelve-year-old Messiah to absorb. FATHER in His wisdom knew the exact amount of reality to reveal. I knew that along My journey He would impart more as I grew in age, experience, and wisdom. The elation of My messianic awakening was beyond words but very humbling to My flesh.

A gust a wind roused Me to My responsibility at home in the village below. It was difficult to leave this place, to reenter the home of clattering plates and bowls as the evening meal was prepared. My eyes were still moist, and My mind was still reeling from the experience of eternal glory.

After supper, I was so thankful when the last candle was extinguished, and baby Simon ended his whimpering with sleep. I lay on My mat, still basking in My afternoon with Father. My soul was still bursting with love, joy, and peace. This had been a taste of My eternal past, and the experience had taken its toll on My human strength, for I was exhausted. My spirit was soaring, but this human body was tired and needed to ease into sleep.

Then the dream unfolded. Father knew this was the perfect window to fill Me with deeper understanding. My spirit was awake while My body slept. I saw this indescribable place of vivid colors and light. Without any explanation, I knew it was the abode of Father. There was no discovery in My dream, for I knew everything about this wondrous place.

Every creature, every living thing, every effervescent drop of water, and every wisp of glory was more than familiar notes of a song, for I had an uninterrupted and complete memory of its very creation.

Then, there was Father and Spirit. Father uttered again, and His thunderous voice echoed across galaxies never to be seen by man. Spirit portrayed the Word declared in eternal, immeasurable time that depicted the Son on earth. The Lamb slain before time and creation portrayed in an eternal capsule that My eternal spirit could absorb. I would bear a cross before I wore a crown.

Father knew this dream was the vehicle for My further understanding, for it would have been difficult for My young clay vessel to digest and comprehend.

He showed Me the summary of the plan of the ages. The

red thread of redemption that ran through the course of earthly centuries interwoven in the history of man. Mankind in their ignorance and iniquity waged war and conflict to garner momentary control of the earth. Men had sought to control others when they had no control over themselves. Futility was in their minds, and corruption was in their souls.

In this imagery of the vision of the night, the Eternal One revealed to the Eternal Son how I was the needle inserted into the tapestry of history, bringing the thread of redemption to the fabric of earthly time. This had to be delivered in the vision of the night as My spirit was open and aware and while My earthly mind slumbered in deep sleep.

I woke to the bustle of Ima in the house, preparing for a new day. And it was a new day indeed. I snuggled deeply into My wool blanket from the chill of the morning, but I felt as if I were floating. My mind was spinning from the filaments of My vision of the night. In the vision, I was the point of God's plan, but now I needed to fetch water in an earthen vessel.

To know is a wonderful thing, but the understanding of that knowledge is overwhelming. I dreamed in glory, awakened in wonder, and began My day as if in another dream. The table and chairs seemed different. Ima's voice, so familiar and kind, was almost strange in an unusual sense. This world now seemed like an intrusion in My dream, even though My eternal purpose was staged in its dust.

I knew. I just knew! My awakening had come, and now it was as if My departure from heaven and My coming to earth had just happened. I knew it had happened more than a decade ago, yet it was so much in the present. My awakening also aroused in Me the greater understanding of the brevity of earthly life compared to the unmeasurable expanse of eternity. I saw Myself in both.

FATHER had unveiled His purpose in Me. This purpose from

before time was now illuminated, not only in My mind but also in the very depths of My spirit.

I was the Lamb slain before time, the Messiah. It was a weighty thought for an earthly youth; however, My eternal spirit sustained Me. From the human side, knowing My purpose propelled Me through the most grievous situations. I had an eternal purpose while walking the roads of a finite world.

It was a heavy load for a young boy with human emotions to bear a heavenly spirit. Just entering manhood, My life was now outlined before Me. In time, the revelation would be a finished masterpiece, filled with colors of power, suffering, and redemption. Father had awakened Me to His purpose in Me. The parentheses from My incarnation until now had faded as if it had never been. I was the fulfillment of Father's complete Word. I was the Alpha and the Omega, the beginning and the end.

Awakened to My purpose, I also knew the stages of My future would be revealed by Father as I went forward. I walked in this world as a man, but the revelation of Father's plan would be fully obvious as I stood in the light of each day. My humanness constrained the all-knowing I had before My coming, but I was confident in Father's guidance and revelation.

The depth of My spirit was filled with oceans of understanding that surged against the shores of My human comprehension. There was a deep aquifer in My spirit filled with waters of eternal knowledge, wisdom, and understanding that Father would mete out as He willed.

Father would fill the reservoirs of My human comprehension from the depths of My spirit as the events of My journey required. He would reveal to Me as I went the necessary understanding in the appropriate time and at the appropriate place.

I was walking in heavenly light yet with My feet on the sand of earth. Father was allowing Me the experience of a man who walked in perfect steps with God. The Messiah had to walk in human sandals. As the Anointed One, I had to experience the anointing of God in human terms. I was not only to be an example of God on the earth; I was also the example of a man filled with the Spirit of God, one who was completely obedient in words and actions. I was One with Him. I was only to speak as He spoke and only to do as He did.

Each day brought a new revelation of FATHER's plan for that day and the immediate future. I was aware of the whole plan, but FATHER unveiled the details as needed. This was the journey of the Messiah as FATHER allowed Me to be God in flesh, but I was also very human. And so I went day by day.

Synagogue was even more intriguing now. Our local elders taught the scriptures on the Sabbath, and when they read from the scroll, it was like hearing My own voice. I heard the voice of the prophets yielding the Word given by Holy Spirit. I could feel the power surge of the Spirit and the heartbeat of the prophet.

Not only did I hear their individual voices, but I also felt their emotions when the Spirit moved upon them. I had sensed the movement of Holy Spirit when the ancients received the Word. I understood the meaning as a man might understand, but I also recognized the nuances of My FATHER's heart.

The Word written was once the Word spoken. A man familiar with an author's voice can often hear his voice upon the reading of his words. When the words are read from the scrolls of the Torah, I can hear the eternal voice of the Author. I AM the Word, the very expression of My FATHER.

This newfound understanding often made Me sad when some twisted My FATHER's Word. It made Me pity the poor soul who misrepresented the truth through pure human ignorance. The mysteries of the Word became as conscious light of understanding to Me. I did not have to strain to understand and search to know; I just knew.

The understanding of My Father's Word and His heart was just obvious to Me. Just as breathing was second nature to a healthy man, so was the inhaling of the *Breath of God*, His Word to Me. Others seemed to struggle to inhale the Word, like a dying man gasping for his last few breaths.

The difficulties of life had become obscure and insignificant in the light of My greater understanding. I was in Father, and Father was in Me. My Father's purpose was streaming through Me, so the difficulties of life were only slight inconveniences. They were as a traveling man stepping over stones in the road with his eyes on a distant destination.

I easily saw that My fellow villagers did not trust Father, though He held their next breath in His hand. If only they knew His love for them, worry would have never touched their hearts. I noticed the birds never worried, for they ended each day with a full belly, not worrying if there would be food tomorrow. Father knew when the smallest of creatures took their first breaths and their last. I walked in perfect peace whether the crops were plentiful or pitiful.

I labored with Abba. He was patient with Me as I learned his trade. His skilled hands would turn pieces of raw wood into useful implements and furniture. I saw the image of My Heavenly Father as I watched My earthly father craft a piece of wood. His creation was useful but far less complex than Our dance of Creation.

I chuckled in amusement when I realized the part I had played in the intricate details of creation, yet while in Joseph's shop, I struggled to cut a straight line with a saw. The simple struggles of men were an experience I had to experience while living in the creation I had brought forth.

FATHER had sent Me from heaven to earth, from eternity to time, from a place of perfection to a fallen world. I was God but living as a man. I was of infinite eternity dwelling in finite time. It was exhilarating to My earthly mind yet also burdensome. We had determined in eternal completeness that My earthly journey would be constrained by the limitations of My earthly existence. Holy Spirit would empower Me to do all FATHER purposed Me to do.

I knew My human existence was different than any other man, past, present, or future. From Adam, all men carried the fallenness from the Garden of Eden. All were born with a corrupt spirit. Though many were noble and some were even called righteous and good, within all was still the corrupt seed of sin. My conception made My being so different. I was born of a virgin woman, so man had not begotten Me; I was the only begotten of God, My FATHER. The source of My flesh was woman, but the source of My spirit was God.

There was not in Me the propensity for sin or rebellion against FATHER. In Me was a propensity for righteousness and total conformity to the desire of FATHER. I would only say what I heard Him say, and I would only do the works I saw Him do.

My gravitation toward righteousness also had a repulsion regarding sin. Everyone I lived among in this world had an attraction to sin and struggled for righteousness.

We knew people would comprehend My coming through a religious prism not consistent with FATHER's truth. There was one primary reason for the Son coming in flesh, and it was embodied in His sacrifice for all sin. However, there were many times in My journey on earth when I had to live and learn as all men did. Above all the tumult of earth, now I lived with the awareness of who I was.

CHAPTER SIX

IMA'S STORY

*Behold the maidservant of the Lord! Let it
be to me according to your word.*

LUKE 1:38

I knew it was wise not to speak about My messianic awareness at this time. My brothers and sisters were too young to even consider the matter. My parents were very perceptive about all their children, so I knew that they may discern some difference in Me. Sacred things need to be held close, and FATHER had instilled in Me the importance of timing. This knowledge of My identity was so profound and eternal that even My close family would have difficulty accepting the gravity of it. It was quite overwhelming to My young human mind as well, but My eternal spirit within Me was steadfast to do the right thing at the right time.

Human souls need the fellowship of others to share the joys and sorrows of life, but this was something so holy. When the struggles of My awareness weighed upon My young heart, I stole away to abide with FATHER. This is where I emptied My heart to FATHER in solitude, and it was such a comfort.

I often asked permission of Abba to retreat beyond the edges of the village to spend the night alone in the outdoors. At first Ima was concerned about Me being alone, but Abba sensed My need and assured her that everything was fine.

I would take a morsel of bread, a blanket, and a fire ember from Ima's fire so I could spend time in solitude with FATHER. These were wonderful times spent in hours of uninterrupted time with FATHER. During these occasions, I received spiritual impartations of strength as well as consolation.

The months rolled by after My awakening, and the world around Me took on an eternal perspective. Everything around Me seemed different, and My viewpoint was often contrary to the norms around Me.

I often had a heavenly sensation permeating My soul. For My young human senses, it was almost overpowering at times. When a wave of revelation would course over Me, it was difficult to concentrate on the task at hand. I frequently had to find an exit from My Nazareth family to get alone with FATHER.

Whenever I accompanied Abba to the nearby city of Sepphoris, there was always a conversation with local men in the marketplace. This is where we received our news of recent events. A recently returned traveler from Jerusalem had news of events to share. It was not unusual for him to tell of the antics of the Roman soldiers with disgust in his voice. He would talk about a Roman soldier conscripting him to carry his bag for mile on a Roman road. When the men thought I was not listening, they would speak of a young girl carried off to the side of the road and violated by the soldiers. Of course, for us Hebrews, there was no recourse to the brutality. We had to bear the load and shame of Roman tyranny.

As the men discussed the oppressive acts, one would eventually speak with yearning in his voice about the coming Messiah. With tears, many old men would bemoan, "When is Messiah coming to rid us of the reproachful oppression?" Often, I was within an arm's length of them, and they would look at Me with pity, viewing Me only as a boy who was destined to inherit the misery of our people.

Prayers were prayed in the synagogue for deliverance. I also heard the longing words of King David read, when he cried out for deliverance in the scrolls of the songs of praise. The yearning hearts were crying for deliverance yet did not know the purpose and timing of FATHER's foretold Messiah.

I readily sensed that Abba and Ima were more than a little concerned about Me. I knew they knew something of My change, but they had not experienced My side of the awareness. There had been prophets who had received amazing revelations from Holy Spirit, but none of the great prophets were the Messiah, the Son of God. The road upon which I walked had never been traveled.

One morning, I heard My parents talking, and I knew they were discussing Me. Their voices were low, hushed, and difficult for Me to discern. FATHER had determined My earthly limitations in this human existence. I received understanding as it needed to be revealed. I was the Son of God, but I had to live in this vessel of clay. I felt My parents' dilemma; it was obvious.

Who of men could understand their situation? They were an ordinary couple in an often-despised village in a corner of Israel under Roman oppression, yet they had the responsibility to steward the young Messiah. FATHER had entrusted this unlearned and common couple with His Son.

My identity and personhood were not so much a secret as they were a treasure to be revealed. There would be times and people for whom the revelation would be simple and straightforward. Other times it would need to be cloaked and hidden. The timing of My Messiahship was of the utmost importance; this FATHER had clearly made known to Me. I was like Ima: I kept these things and pondered them in My heart. My time would come, but the timing would be FATHER's, not mine.

The quiet meetings of Abba and Ima continued on and off for weeks as though they were planning some event. I could hear their soft tones in the early mornings before My siblings rose like little roosters to declare a new day.

One day, unexplained, Abba declared he was taking all the children to visit a relative in a nearby village. They packed a little food in a bag and a skin of water for the dusty journey. He told Me to stay and help Ima with the chores since I was the oldest. I was quite happy with the arrangement. The noise of the family would be lightened by the absence of My loud clan. And I loved to be alone with Ima. We had a special connection, and we loved each other's company.

The children were excited to go on a little excursion. They also knew the family of Tobiah would have special treats for them; they were known for their gracious hospitality. With the sudden clamor of rushing about, My siblings readied themselves for the journey. Soon the little band of giggling girls and scuffling boys were out the door and gone.

I asked Ima what she needed Me to do first. She gave Me three copper coins and told Me to buy one of the fresh melons our neighbors sold in her little stand next to her house. Also, she needed a jug of water from the well on My way back.

Off I went for My early morning chores. It was a beautiful day. The sun had risen just a little from the east by southern horizon. I could hear the birds giving their morning song from the branches. The usual sounds of the village came to My ears: a few barking dogs, the clatter of households beginning their work, faint voices, and the delightful chatter of children. It was a wonderful day.

I was also glad for the absence of My little clan. It would be a good opportunity for solitude and quietness. A little uninterrupted time with Ima, which I always cherished. With Abba away, My workload in the workshop was limited. I had only one task to complete for tomorrow's delivery.

Mariam greeted My arrival with a smile and a "shalom." She had some wonderful looking melons and helped Me pick a big ripe one with the thump of her finger. I paid for our treat and stopped at the well to retrieve a jug of water. The neck of the jug had a small rope fastened to it so I could carry it slung from My shoulder.

Upon arriving home, I put all My chore items on the floor. Ima poured the water into a large basin, into which she lowered the melon for cooling. The refreshing treat would be for later. Thinking about it made My mouth water.

She urged Me to finish the task in the workshop and said when I returned, we would enjoy the juicy melon together. The day before, Abba and I had carefully cut and hewn the pieces for two chairs. We had fashioned the joints with mortises and tenons with the chisels that Abba protected like gold. Proper metal to hold an edge was hard to find and expensive, but the good tools made this type of work possible. Abba was known throughout our little region for his wonderful joinery.

I enjoyed working by Myself. The solitude was peaceful and quiet. I assembled the chairs with a little glue Abba had put in a little earthen vessel. When we were in Egypt, he had learned the process of boiling animal skins to get this substance for keeping the wood joints tight and strong. Sometimes he would mix it with tar pitch or the resin from trees.

The chairs looked good, and I hoped Abba would be pleased with My work. They would dry overnight and be ready for delivery tomorrow. Hopefully, he would allow Me to make the delivery since I had finished them.

Upon finishing My work, I remembered there was a cool melon waiting to be sliced. There was nothing like the completion of a task with a sweet reward waiting!

Ima was just taking some flatbread from the domed griddle that was heated by coals. She had prepared a small vessel with olive oil, a bit of sour wine, and an even smaller amount of sesame oil blended with a pinch of salt and spices. This was special, as if for a guest. I asked who was coming for the meal. She smiled and said, "You!"

"Oh, Ima, sesame oil, bread, and a melon just for Me!"

Her face was beaming. "Yes, just for You, my sweet son!"

This was a special treat for an evening meal, but now the sun was straight overhead. I knew Ima had something on her mind. This noonday meal was when all the neighbors would be taking a midday reprieve from the heat in their homes or under a special tree. We would be undisturbed.

We thanked God for the bread and ate it with little talk. I loved Ima's flatbread, and it was especially good with the added sesame oil mix.

After the bread, she asked Me to cut the melon. Its red flesh, juicy texture, and sweetness was so delicious. It was a wonderful dessert and a beautiful time with just Ima and Me. After we had eaten our fill, we both leaned back and sighed. Ima's face shone with sweet contentment. She loved being with her firstborn, and I cherished these few moments with just her.

After a pause from our light conversation, she became serious and smiled a nervous smile. She broke the brief silence with a question: "Jesus, your Abba and I have been concerned about you lately. You seem a little distracted and keep to Yourself more. Are You well?"

"Yes, Ima. I am fine!" I replied.

She was not exactly satisfied with My answer. I countered her questioning look by saying, "Yes, really. I am fine. I have been talking much with My Heavenly FATHER."

As if correcting Me, she said, "You mean you have been praying to Adonai, yes?"

"Well, yes, praying but more than praying, actually! We have been talking. He has been talking with Me about My purpose. He has been showing Me in detail about His plan and purpose for Me on earth."

Tears began to roll down her face, replacing her sweet smile. When she found her composure, she asked a cloaked question that we both understood: "So You know who You are?"

"Yes, Ima. I know who I AM! FATHER has shown Me who I AM and His purpose for Me. I AM the SON OF GOD!

She turned a little pale at My statement, followed by a flush of redness. With an awkward look on her face, she asked, "What all do you know? I mean, how much do you know?"

"Ima, it is difficult with words to describe this to you. I know I AM from Him, but FATHER has shown Me that many things are not yet fully in view. FATHER will reveal as I go forward. I must adhere to His timing. I can only do what He shows Me and say what I hear Him say."

Ima, still softly crying, looked at the ground. Then she asked, "Do you know how you came about?"

"I only know that Abba is not My true father and you are innocent of any ill happenings; the details My FATHER has left to you. It is your story to tell. Whenever you feel it is proper, I am ready to listen and learn."

Ima wiped the tears from her eyes and smiled a slight smile as she glanced at the door to confirm we were alone. She looked relieved but burdened with the task of unraveling her long-held story.

Then she began: "Joseph and I had committed to a betrothal

to be married. I was so excited to begin my young life as a wife with such a good man. Your grandfather Jacob and Joseph had spoken with my father, making all the marriage arrangements. After the arrangements came the preparation for the coming wedding.

"One day as I was gathering firewood from the hillside behind our house, a strange thing happened. Unexpectedly and unannounced, this powerful angel stood before me. His name was Gabriel. He called me highly favored and blessed and said that the LORD was with me.

"I was so scared! Why would an angel appear to me? Why was I favored by God? I was just a common village girl in this lowly village of Nazareth. I was trembling with fear and in great awe of this angelic being. It was a frightful experience!

"The angel told me not to be afraid because God held me in high favor. Then he told me I was to conceive and bear a Son whose name would be Jesus. He told me that You would be great and called the Son of the Most High God. He said You would receive the throne of King David and that You would reign forever, for Your kingdom would be endless.

"I was so confused because I was not yet married to Joseph. We had not come together as husband and wife. I was an innocent village girl, but my mother had explained the ways of life to me. So I told the angel, 'How can I bear a child since I have not known a man intimately?'

"I remember the angel taking his eyes from me and looking heavenward. He told me the Holy Spirit would come upon me, the power of God would overshadow me, and this Holy Child would be called the Son of God. He told me of Elizabeth's miraculous conception of John in her old age, who was now six months into her time with child. He also said that with God nothing was impossible.

"This was more than I could comprehend at first. It was like a tangle of thread in my mind that was difficult to untangle. I only knew to accept what God had spoken through the angel. I had questions, but I had no doubt. I simply replied to the angel, 'Behold the maidservant of the Lord! Let it be to me according to your word' (Luke 1:38). Then the angel left as quickly as he came."

My Father had left this story for Ima to tell. As she unfolded her mystery, I kept my eyes closed. When she recounted the details, it was revealed in My spirit as if it was presently happening. I could see the scene as if before My natural eyes. Not only did I see the scene, but I also immediately knew Ima's thoughts and emotions as that teenage bearer of the Son of God.

She paused, and I looked up into her eyes. Tears continued to course down her cheeks, and she sobbed the cry of relief. Tears came to My eyes as well. I embraced her, and she sobbed and sobbed while melting into My embrace.

Finally, I pulled away from her loving arms and held her at arm's length while looking deep into her dark, moist eyes. "Oh, Ima. This is all true. I know! You were such a brave young lady. My Father chose well. He chose you of all women to be My mother. Thank you for choosing to be My Ima!"

She had been crying, but now the deep well of her emotion flooded even more, and she wept with deep release of her spirit. The wave of her emotions, held for many years, finally broke through the gates of her soul. I held her again and allowed every drop to pour forth. Then when her weeping ceased, she laughed a soft, embarrassed laugh and said, "I did not choose You. All these things just happened."

"Oh yes, Ima. You did choose! You said, 'Let it be according to Your will.' Yes, you chose Me, and We chose you!"

Now she smiled a knowing and relieved smile.

Changing the conversation from her, I asked, "So what about Abba?"

Ima answered with an exasperated smile. "What about Joseph? What about my mother and father? I had to tell them first. A betrothed couple cannot talk about such things."

We both laughed.

She continued, "My mother and father were quite bewildered. Nothing like this was possible in their minds. They knew I was a good girl, and I could see their minds trying to find a time I had been alone with Joseph or with another man.

"I saw they wanted to believe me, but it was also a very difficult story to accept. They had doubts. I knew it was a great struggle for them. My father just shook his head and said, 'I must talk with Joseph about these matters.'

"He went the next day and told Joseph I was with child and about my claims of a message from an angel. Joseph also found it difficult to believe. He told my father he needed time to consider all these claims. Father said Joseph felt confused, betrayed, and shamed. And oh how that broke my heart! It was so painful to think about all the trouble I had caused them.

"The next day, Joseph and his father visited my father as I stayed hidden in our little house. Joseph had made the decision to keep all this as quiet as possible. He would give me a certificate of divorcement and the family could send me away to a distant relative, at least until the baby was born. Then I was to live out my life in shame and get by the best I could. He even offered to not contest the dowry he had paid, but my father declined his offer. My father said that in these circumstances, it would not be right for the bride's family to keep the dowry. Joseph was and is such a good man."

I smiled and agreed, "Yes, Ima. He is a very good man with a kind heart."

Ima rejoined her story: "Joseph was a good-hearted man, and there was mercy in his plan. He could have called me before the elders and called for a public stoning, as I was seen as an adulterous woman with an unlawful child. This was all according to the Torah.

"There was no doubt in my mind at the reality of the angel's appearance and words. I of all people knew I had not been with a man. Knowing that it was such an unbelievable story made the doubtful looks bearable, but they were still painful. My poor mother and father. I felt so sorry for them. They were very courageous and as merciful as they knew to be.

"I was devastated at the news, but I knew this was a strange story indeed. I prepared to leave my mother and father before my child within me grew to a size that would be hard to hide. My mother and father decided I should go to our kinfolks in the hill country of Judah, just west of Jerusalem in the city of Ein Karem.

"My long journey of more than a week was made with trusted travelers. Our travel took us south. The couple with whom I would stay were a kinswoman named Elizabeth and her husband, Zacharias. I was happy to go to her home. She was a very kindhearted woman. She was known to be barren for many years, but the angel said she was six months with child. I did not tell this to my parents but knew it to be true. They had no idea she was with child.

"The journey was grueling. I was sick many mornings because I was with child. The sickness made the travel even more difficult. There was also the added burden of trying to hide my condition.

"I was so happy to finally arrive in the city where Elizabeth lived. It had been the last Passover since we had seen each other. Zacharias met me at the gate. He seemed not able to speak for some reason. He motioned with his hand for me to follow him. Then he opened the door, pointing inside for me to enter. Since he could not speak, I thought it best to announce my arrival, 'Shalom Elizabeth!'

"Immediately she began to speak as if a prophesy, 'Blessed are you among women, and blessed is the fruit of your womb!'" (Luke 1:42).

"Elizabeth continued to speak in the same prophetic tone: 'Why am I privileged to have the mother of my Lord visit me? My baby leaped for joy in my womb at the sound of your voice. You believed. Adonai has blessed you for believing. The Lord will certainly bring to fulfillment all things He has told you.'

"It was a thrilling moment of affirmation. Up to this point, no one believed me. The Spirit of God moved upon me, and I glorified God with a song. You may have heard me sing this song in the mornings, yes?"

"Oh yes, Ima. I know this song you often sing. I love to listen to the words, and I enjoy the melody also. It is a beautiful song filled with glory to Father from His special servant's heart," I answered.

She smiled at My words and continued her story: "I planned to stay with Elizabeth to help her with the baby and housekeeping. At three months, I felt compelled to return to Nazareth, not knowing what good or bad awaited me there.

"I left for Nazareth just before her baby was born. Soon after I arrived in Nazareth, one day, Joseph appeared at our home unannounced. He spoke with my father at the gate of our little yard. He insisted he needed to say things to my father, mother, and me. My father protested that this was not proper, but Joseph was very persistent. Finally, my father consented.

"We four gathered, and my parents sent the other children away. When the house was cleared of young ears, my father beckoned Joseph to speak. I could see Joseph was extremely nervous but also determined.

"Joseph began, 'I know Mary is known to be a righteous girl, but her news was just too difficult to believe. How can a young lady be with child without the company of a man? As these things weighed heavily on my mind, four nights ago, as I was sleeping, an angel appeared to me in a dream. He told me not to be afraid to take Mary for my wife. I would have come sooner, but I did not know Mary had returned until yesterday.'

"We all were surprised at this change. Then Joseph continued to relay the events of his dream: 'The angel confirmed this child's conception was by the Holy Spirit. His name is to be Jesus. The angel spoke of Isaiah's prophesy of the virgin being with child. Immanuel, God with Us, describes His being. I now know that Mary is this prophesied virgin, and this child is God With Us in her womb. This marriage can go forward as planned. I will be the husband of Mary and the guardian father of this appointed Son.'

"I remember this moment so well. I was so relieved and so grateful that God had sent His messenger to me and to Joseph. My father and mother were relieved but still overwhelmed by all the events. They finally believed me and my unbelievable story.

"My admiration for Joseph was beyond words. My heart was so full of love for him. I thanked God for all the changed minds. Joseph is such a righteous and good man. God surely chose him too."

I smiled at Ima. "Yes. We chose him too!"

We both laughed with tears of joy. I hugged her again, and she smiled with relief and peace.

She asked one more question: "What now?"

I told her, "It is not My time now, but one day it will be. Until then, we take one day and one step at a time until the time appointed. Father will reveal to Me when He chooses."

She smiled in agreement and stood to leave.

I took her by the hand, causing her to pause. "Ima, I know this journey with Me has had moments of difficulty and the future will have more days of trials. But you must know, My FATHER chose you for this journey. You are highly favored! Never doubt the destiny of My FATHER, regardless of what a day brings."

She smiled in agreement and didn't say another word. FATHER had chosen a strong woman for My mother. I was so thankful for her, and I could see the courage and strength of her heart.

We smiled and parted to do chores around the house. Abba and My brood of siblings soon returned and devoured the remaining melon as the sun was nearing the western horizon.

That night when My siblings were asleep, I lay on My mat and pulled the blanket under My chin as the chill of the night came to give us a reprieve from the heat. In another corner of our house, I could hear the muffled voices of Ima and Abba. She was relating the earlier conversation with Me. The blanket keeping Me warm was woven from the fibers of nearby sheep. FATHER was using the threads of our small family to weave a beautiful tapestry that one day would reveal a glorious picture of FATHER's purpose and plan on the earth.

CHAPTER SEVEN

YOUNG SCHOLAR

Did you not know that I must be about My Father's business?

LUKE 2:49

My siblings and I were excited about going to Jerusalem for the Passover. The trek of the week-long journey and the busyness of crowded Jerusalem was a break from the mundane life in Nazareth. For My young siblings and I, it was a wonderful excursion. My parents were not as enthusiastic, but their closely held faith urged them on. The grown-ups loved the religious aspects of the Passover, but the journey was tiring, sometimes dangerous, and always costly.

The roads were more crowded than usual because of the upcoming festival. Our journey along the road would be with other families for company and protection along the way. The usual campsites were at the locations of wells or other water sources, where we could replenish our waterskins and water for cooking meals. Our overnight camps were filled with meals, stories from old men, and cries from tired toddlers. Sometimes there was an occasional song, but most people were too tired for merriment.

We all dreamed of Jerusalem, but I felt a different tug than from past years. The journey to Jerusalem this year was more than youthful desire for adventure. I was not traveling to Jerusalem; I was being drawn to Jerusalem. This spiritual pull was not by an external force but by an internal surge of knowing that it was more than a capital city of My people; it was a place of destiny for Me, My people, and the world.

The days of walking dusty roads, drinking strange water, and enduring sore legs were coming to an end as we saw the great city rising from the horizon. The houses on the outskirts were becoming more clustered together when we drew nearer. We saw the walls separating it from the world outside. A gate welcomed all the weary pilgrims from near and far.

Ah, Jerusalem, the center of our Jewish faith and known to Me as the center of the earth. Millenniums in the future, the world would flock here. I dared not speak of it, for My FATHER, who is all wisdom, knew all about the right time. I only spoke of events to come as He revealed them to Me.

We made our way through the bustling city, past the street merchants peddling their goods, and weary pilgrims gathering supplies. Abba said we would be staying with Ima's kinsman, Micah. He and his family were also hosting several pilgrim families like ours. Micah had a larger than normal house within the city walls. It had a small courtyard that would be perfect for several families to share. There would be enough room for all of us, but we would be sleeping shoulder to shoulder on woven mats.

It was such a relief to turn down a quieter street, knowing our journey was ending in a few hundred paces. Micah was waiting outside under the shade of a sycamore tree. The smile on his face and the "shalom" on his lips revealed the generosity in his heart. We had finally arrived.

Salome, his wife, brought water for us to refresh ourselves

and returned to her cooking fire. It took just a little time for us to renew old acquaintances and find our familiar spot in someone else's home.

We were not too surprised to see My mother's kinsman Elizabeth and her son, John, whose father, Zacharias, had died the previous year. Elizabeth seemed too old to have a son not even a year older than Me. I could see the sparkle in Elizabeth's eyes as she looked at Ima and then at Me, as if the two had a secret that no one else knew. Their embrace was intermingled with giggles of joy. I was in on their secret but went about My activities as if it was all normal.

It had been a year since I had seen John. He had grown a lot. His voice was beginning to deepen, and the darkening fuzz on his face revealed the coming of a man. He had always been of the serious sort with no nonsense about him, even as a young boy. There was a contemplative look in his eye and a serious tone to his voice. He loved the Torah and the Prophets and had memorized much of the scrolls.

He and I were quite different, although there was a strong bond when we were together. The distance between our homes was a long journey, so we seldom visited. When we came together after a long absence, the connection was seamless. He was always excited to see Me for no outward reason, but there was a look in his eyes that said more than he expressed.

Our bond was drawn from a well, deeper than ordinary kinship, even though he was not aware of it. His understanding remained veiled for now. I knew we were fibers of the same thread that FATHER was weaving through the history of the world. He felt the connection, not knowing the why, but one day on a riverbank, this budding prophet would flower and bear fruit.

I was always filled with wonder at our Hebrew holidays. Passover was especially grand. This year, Abba and the heads of our families purchased a lamb to be shared. During our celebration, we sang, prayed, and shared stories of God's deliverance. One story usually told was God's deliverance by Moses from four centuries of bondage in Egypt. The meal resembled the original Passover, with unleavened bread, bitter herbs, and roasted lamb.

I knew this year's Passover was going to be different for Me. Most of the tired pilgrims were going through the religious motions with hardly a thought of its true story. Even those whose religious fervor was keen saw nothing but the past. This year I saw the future.

The main element to the Passover meal is the lamb. It commemorates the night of the Passover in Egypt when all the firstborn except those behind the door anointed with the blood of the lamb died in the night. The blood was painted on the doorposts and the lintel above the door. Those inside the barrier of blood ate the same lamb from which the blood came. It was roasted in fire and eaten with unleavened bread and bitter herbs.

The lamb was to be unblemished and a male of the first year. As we gathered in the household of our kindred, we were cloistered behind closed doors. For this solemn moment, all the clamor of the world was beyond the door. We were alone with the Passover lamb whose blood in the premiere Passover had been smeared on the entrance.

In our time, the lamb was killed between the two evenings of the sun, after the evening sacrifice. Between the two evenings was when the sun began its descent after high noon until it finally set in the evening. In the time of Moses, "between the two evenings" was between sunset and full darkness when three stars could be seen. Our people considered it a new day when they could see three medium-size stars in the night sky.

The Passover meal began in the evening just before the sun set and continued into the new day of evening after the stars showed.

Our celebration meal would begin at the close of one day and continue into the new day, taking several hours.

It was more than a meal; it was a celebration of songs, historical stories, prayers, tastings of foods, eating, and the ceremonial drinking of four cups of wine.

I helped Ima and My other family members with some of the final preparations. Ima was always leading the way when it came to hospitality and serving. She seemed to never stop working. Her hands and feet were a whirlwind of activity. I was amazed at her heart of service and stamina.

There was much preparation for this highly celebrated Passover. The lamb was butchered and cooked. Then there was the preparation of the other dishes of unleavened bread, sweet condiments, green herbs, and bitter herbs, as well as the wine.

When we gathered this evening, no one was aware of the significance of this night. They thought only of the history of our people's deliverance from the horrible grip of slavery in Egypt. I could sense it would be a different Passover than any in My earthly past. FATHER had purposely limited My understanding so it would unfold in time as with the others. I just knew something was brewing in the spiritual realm.

Micah was the head of the home we shared, so he urged everyone to begin to assemble for the meal as daylight neared its end. All the food was arranged on the designated rug in the middle of the large room. There were ample cushions for the adults and rugs for the children. Everything was beautifully arranged. An air of expectancy filled the home.

Just as noted in the Torah, the lamb could be shared by families, causing all the lamb to be consumed before sunrise. Any meat that remained was to be burned in the fire. Micah took the place of host, and Abba was seated at his right. We all were positioned around the meal.

We began by singing hymns of praise and deliverance. Prayers were offered, and we ate the meal.

One tradition we included was a symbolic cup of wine on the table for Elijah. It represented his coming to announce the arrival of the Messiah. FATHER flooded My being with the vision of the future prophet presently sitting at the table with us. John, the son of Zacharias, one day would proclaim the coming Messiah and be known as John the Baptist. Tonight, at this table, on this Passover, was John, the Elijah-like prophet and forerunner of the Messiah. Across from him, I sat as the to-be-announced Messiah, "the Lamb slain from the foundation of the world" (Rev. 13:8). What a glorious and prophetic Passover!

The weight of this night immediately engulfed Me as we continued with the meal. The Lamb without blemish and in His first year was in our midst, and it was Me. I was entering the first year as the "son of the Law," and My soul was untarnished by sin.

When our combined family ate the lamb, suddenly it became more than a morsel of meat. Waves of visions were sent through My spirit as I tasted it. I felt a taste of the grief that the Lamb of God would bear.

No one yet knew, and for a moment, I felt alone and rejected. I could sense the feeling of damnation, though I had never sinned. Tears coursed down My young face. I sensed the sacrifice of rejection to come and the price to be paid for sin. I did not feel physical pain but rather a grieving in My soul. FATHER allowed Me a taste, but the full measure would be felt many years from now.

Then I saw a glimpse of My eternal past, with the Lamb as though He had been slain. He was standing in the aura of glory, having opened the seals and revealed the redemptive plan. He was Me! The weight of this moment filled our room, but only I understood the magnitude of the moment. Tears poured from My eyes as My spirit overflowed My soul.

Abba looked at Me. He was quite puzzled yet said nothing. Ima and Elizabeth looked at Me and then at John.

John had tears in his eyes also but from a surge of the Spirit of God, not by understanding. Our tears mingled together in the moment, just like our lives and destiny intertwined in FATHER's plan. We were just boys at the crossing of manhood, mostly smooth-faced yet each with a destiny.

I knew that Elizabeth and Ima had some knowledge of our significance, but the depth of it was veiled to them. I also knew that Abba had some understanding of My appointment with God. The rest of the family was curiously moved but unknowing altogether. It was a holy moment in this Jerusalem home while we reclined at the Passover meal.

Ima and Elizabeth began to sob. The mood swept the room, as all were emotionally touched. We continued to eat of the lamb moistened with warm tears. This night in Jerusalem, Hebrews celebrated their release from a pharaoh's chains. Yet in our celebration, we in one way or another celebrated the Lamb in our midst, the Lamb who would take away the sins of the world, and His forerunner prophet.

The meal and celebration continued with touching moments like one would sense at an eighth-day circumcision or a funeral. The naming of a child and his death combined in one holy observance. No other Passover meal would be as important as this one and My last one.

After the celebration, I retired to My sleeping mat, relieved and reeling at the same time. This was much to take in, even for a twelve-year-old Messiah. When sleep came, so did My dreams, and angels comforted My soul while I slept.

The next morning as we ate some fruit and leftover bread, the mood in the house was somber. Everyone went about their usual activities like nothing had happened the night before. However, there was an air of wonder and even confusion for some.

I sensed an intensity in My spirit when our time in Jerusalem came to an end. Our family prepared to depart for Nazareth as soon as the weeklong Feast of Unleavened Bread, which immediately followed Passover, ended.

We completed our final week of worship, and Abba and Ima made final preparations for our return to Nazareth. Our entourage of family and fellow villagers would travel back the next morning. The journey homeward would be almost like a continuation of the celebration, except for the tired feet and sore legs.

Everyone seemed excited about going home. The intensity I had felt during and after Passover returned, causing Me to be drawn to the temple. This was a special place, as FATHER made it to be. We all knew this temple was built by Zerubbabel and renovated by King Herod. It was grand, but it was not the temple that Solomon had erected.

What attracted Me was not the great edifice but rather the Presence. My family had brought Me here a dozen times since My birth, but this trip was very different. The Presence had an unseen and unheard sway on Me. It was like a homing pigeon being drawn to her roost or a migrating bird to its nesting grounds. I had known the Presence of FATHER even in Nazareth, but this was an appointment with His purpose and My destiny.

I slipped away from our dwelling and made My way through the dusty and crowded streets. The high walls and the temple itself seemed to reach into the heavens. It was a glorious sight in this earthly realm, even for those who did not believe.

Upon entering the outer courtyard, I saw a group of scholarly gentlemen gathered under a shade tree. They were vigorously debating some issue. I drew closer to the gathering and heard their discussion, which was centered on the writings of Isaiah.

They were debating about the Coming One, who they supposed Isaiah had foretold. They quoted from Isaiah's words about the man of sorrows.

I squeezed between two hefty teachers as one man droned on and on about his speculation concerning the man of sorrows. The scene affected Me as if I had suddenly surprised local gossips talking about Me. They were oblivious to My presence, for I was just another curious child. Until I spoke!

When there was a pause for air, I asked a simple question from the passage: "Why did the people turn their faces from Him? The scripture so plainly says, 'And we hid, as it were, our faces from Him; He was despised, and we did not esteem Him'" (Isa. 53:3).

Then, with unseen irony, they who turned their faces toward Me would one day be those who turned their faces away. On this day, I was only an inquisitive boy among the scholars. I was only a pea-sized pebble to them, but one day I would be the stone that the builders will reject.

They all turned toward Me, not believing that a young lad would even be interested in their bloviated discussion. They were surprised to hear My profound question that even they had not known to ask. One asked, "Boy, what did you ask?"

I repeated My question: "Why did the people turn their faces from Him?"

There was a moment of awkward silence only broken by a chuckle from the eldest, followed by, "Boy, what an insightful question from such a lad." The others were still taken aback. Their eyes were taking in My face, but one day I knew they would look away as the scripture foretold.

One of the old scholars cleared his throat and ventured an answer: "Well, no doubt in that day when Messiah appears, some of the reprobates of Israel will reject Him and choose to not follow, so some will choose to look away."

They all joined in chorus: "Oh yes, some will not believe in the Messiah."

Another piped in, "But we all are longing and praying for the Messiah to come. When He comes, we will be like Elijah, declaring His appearance to the people of Israel."

After the awkwardness wore away, I asked them many other questions, which they were eager to answer. Their answers were informed from the scriptures, but I sensed their desire was to elevate their own importance rather than for the glory of FATHER.

When they saw I was learned in the scriptures and had insight beyond My years, they begin to ask Me questions. They were amazed at My understanding and perception of the scriptures. I was amazed how these men were so knowledgeable about the Torah and the Prophets yet so distant from FATHER. To them, the scriptures were a history lesson and a rule book to follow, not a living Word from God.

What surprised them the most was My intimate understanding of FATHER. I saw even by their strained faces that some of My understanding was out of their sphere of comprehension. I knew they had more questions than they asked, but they were ashamed to consult a simple boy.

Our discussion lasted all day. One of who showed more interest in My opinions than the others was a younger member of the group. He invited Me to lodge with him so he could quiz Me more. He and his wife were wonderful hosts. His wife served the most delicious food I had ever eaten. They served Me some very choice cuts of meat cooked in amazing spices. The bread they served was cooked from the finest of flour. While I enjoyed the delicious food, I thought, *Oh, so this is the food of rich people!*

The discussion lasted for days. I was amused at the amount of scholarly nonsense that some covered up by many words. It was evident that they were whitewashed tombs filled with the corruption of the dead. They had corrupted the Torah by the addition of their traditions, which complicated the simplicity of My Father's Word. This was one of My first encounters with religious scholars, and I knew it would not be My last.

These learned scholars were exasperated when I explained that the whole of the law was contained in just a few phrases about loving God with all our hearts, souls, minds, and strength, and loving our neighbors as ourselves. Their eyes showed disbelief, and their faces revealed their hearts. They had missed the simple truths of Father's Word.

At first, they viewed Me as an anomaly in small sandals, but the more our discussions were prolonged, the more I could sense their annoyance with "the boy." By the time Ima and Abba found Me, they were ready to be rid of the boy scholar. The men remained amazed at My questions and My answers to their questions. The surprised looks on their faces were obvious when they saw that My parents were ordinary village people. I could hear the question in their minds: *How could this boy know so much since he is from very ordinary stock?*

My parents were very upset with Me because I had been missing for four days. Mother told Me, "Son, why have You treated us like this? We were so anxious about Your whereabouts and Your safety!"

I knew I was safe in Father's destiny, so her deep concern was not shared by Me. So I told her, "Did you not know that I must be about My Father's business?" (Luke 2:49).

Mother did not wholly understand My reply, but she let it be and only said, "Let's be going. We have a long journey."

It would be a long journey, indeed. These scholars and their kind I would meet again, not as the son of Joseph but as the Son of God.

Some of the caravan had continued without us to Nazareth.

A few of our kin had waited for the "boy rabbi" and His anxious family. I received My share of, "Where have you been?"

My mother shushed the too-curious. She wanted no more talk about it.

After a little supper, we settled down for the night. I loved the moments before sleep as everyone was quiet and the darkness was like a curtain from questioning eyes. Lying on My mat and peering at the stars through the opening of the tent, I revisited the moments of our time in Jerusalem. It was a deepening of My understanding of FATHER's plan. Many things that have been previously blurred in My mind were suddenly coming into focus.

I was thankful FATHER's mercies were new every morning so that with the dawn of a new day, the questions finally ceased. The busyness of breaking camp and the weariness of travel soon put My scholarly sojourn in Jerusalem behind us. The journey to Nazareth was uneventful, and the conversations were of mundane things.

Our trip was a long walk on dusty roads with the usual greetings with strangers along the way. It was interesting to see sights outside of our everyday Nazareth, but it was also good to be going home to our usual life in our village town.

CHAPTER EIGHT

APPRENTICE CARPENTER

Is this not the carpenter, the Son of Mary, and brother of James, Joses, Judas, and Simon? And are not His sisters here with us?

MARK 6:3

In My early days, there were siblings born into My family almost every two years. My brothers were James the secondborn, Joses, Simon, and Jude. My sisters were Maya, Elana, Adina, interspersed among the boys. Adina was the last child born before Abba died.

James was a little stubborn but not rebellious. He was physically strong and agile. Joses had a lot of energy and could find fun in anything. Simon was much like Joses but a bit more serious about the trade of carpentry; he loved to work with his hands. We all knew he would exceed the skill of our father as he matured and grew in the trade. Jude was very smart and logical, even as a young man.

My beautiful and giggly sisters brought great joy to our family. They loved Me so much and appreciated My brotherly attention. Since I was their oldest brother, they gave Me more respect than the other boys nearest My age. My sisters' eyes were coal black and could pour tears from the deep well of their hearts at the telling of a sad story or at the death of a near neighbor. Their hearts were so tender, just like Ima's. All the females in My family had soft and tender hearts, although they were also strong and stable.

Males were treasured in our culture, and a man's strength was measured in the number of his sons. Our forefather Jacob called Reuben, his firstborn son, "the beginning of my strength" (Gen. 49:3). My brothers were strong in body, mind, and resolve. My sisters were strong in matters of the heart. They were the best examples of our kind on the earth. Ima was always teaching the girls the skills of an Israelite woman and the expectancy of modesty in our religion and culture.

I loved them all. I watched over them as most older brothers cared for their siblings. We played in the yard and helped with simple chores. I wrestled with My little brothers and played make-believe with My little sisters. Life in childhood seemed like an eternity. My childhood emotions and logic did not track the turning of days. We all lived in the moment and in childhood innocence, trusting our parents for our next morsel of bread and a roof over our heads.

I treasured My sisters. They rarely challenged Me and were never in competition with Me, except in play. My sisters simply loved Me, and I loved them. The familial care to some of My female followers in the future would remind Me of the relationship I had with My sisters. When FATHER made woman, He made a wonderful creature to balance the masculinity of the male. In My sisters and mother, I witnessed up close the wisdom of FATHER's creation of the human female.

Once when I was sitting between Ima and Abba, I grasped their hands and held them in comparison. Abba's hands were calloused from wood, hammers, and saws. His hands in My young mind were fiercely strong, like the hands of Samson, who had killed a lion.

Ima's hands were smaller and soft. They were strong in a feminine way from the many household chores, but they were also strikingly beautiful. I loved to watch her skillfully knead bread like an artist molding clay. She did it without thinking, kneading the dough softly to just the right consistency. Her almost unconscious work was learned through the many measures of meal passing through her hands over the short course of her life.

I loved when she touched My face. She would allow her little finger to drag a furrow over My cheek. Her touch was a caress of love warming My young tender heart. My finished work on Earth would one day crush her precious heart, which would then be refreshed as My purpose came into clearer focus.

Through the years, My mother's early shame was softened by the passing of time and My earthly father's love. In My early childhood, I knew nothing of her personal sacrifice with My unusual conception. While in My eternal state before My conception, I knew her pain and witnessed the whole encounter with Gabriel and all the related events. However, FATHER folded it all away from My consciousness at My conception, to be revealed later.

It was one thing to bear the shame of guilt from wrongdoing but quite another to be innocent and bear its grief. She was innocent and had been obedient to God while bearing the glances of the other villagers and the occasional sharp-tongued accusation from an insensitive neighbor. It was difficult to be scrutinized in a strict moral culture. Ima bore it all from an inner strength of knowing the true declaration of the angel Gabriel. I was inspired by her strength and courage when I encountered the world as an adult.

In a culture like ours, some things were not discussed openly.

My family went about our lives with the day-to-day toil of life. Often when a sensitive subject or situation arose, the gazes of Ima and Abba would meet and convey a message without a word. Coming into My teenager years, I would decipher the little nuanced glances between My parents when a subject near to My conception arose.

Abba and Ima gained back most, if not all, the respect they had lost upon My unusual entry into flesh. Their consistent lives and righteous living among our friends and family erased many memories. I saw their strong resolve to plow headlong into life and prove their critics wrong by a life well lived. Those who bow low before God walk tall among men. Nothing proves your worth like the love you share with others. We knew from the Torah that loving God and our neighbors was at the heart of living a life pleasing to God. My family exemplified this basic premise of My FATHER's Word.

Every day Abba would lead us in the *Shema* prayer. On the Sabbath, we faithfully attended the local synagogue. The words of the Torah were often repeated during our daily activities. Situations of life were filtered through the Word of God when questions arose on how to live in this world.

My mother was kind and gentle. She consistently corrected her children when they became too rowdy or complained about a chore. My siblings knew I was an obedient son and never suspected I was one from beyond. When I was in deep contemplation, Ima only prodded Me when she needed something done. I had a reputation for being a dreamy-eyed child, looking off into the distance with a deep thought on My mind.

Sometimes I would catch of glimpse of Ima staring at Me for no reason. My mother thought much but said little. She kept things to herself and pondered the deep and hard-to-understand prophesies in her heart. There was much to think about as she shepherded the Lamb of God. Her concerns were not only about My future but also about how it would affect the rest of the family. Life is an unfolding of time, one-fold each day until the whole is seen. As I became older, we talked about some of these things, although as a child, I was treated the same as My brothers and sisters.

Ima was a faithful daughter to our grandparents and cared for them as they aged. My grandparents on My father's side lived next door. Abba had built our house on the parcel of his inheritance.

Ima's parents were not far away, only about a half of a Sabbath day's journey to the south. Ima's people were shepherds, and her mother wove wool blankets to stretch the income from the sheep. The blanket I slept under was made by her hands. I carried one of her blankets on My journey through life, eventually leaving it to one of My faithful disciples.

Papa Jacob was a carpenter also and had taught his son Joseph the trade. Our people closely followed the occupation of their fathers. Even as an old man, My grandfather helped in the work until he was too feeble. Abba fully supported his parents when age crept upon them. He also helped with Ima's parents even though most of their help came from their sons.

When age made it impossible for My grandfather and grandmother to do even daily tasks, Abba built quarters adjoining our home to give his parents greater care. He used the materials salvaged from their old house to build a lean-to room onto our home. Their old house had become very rickety, so it was time. It seemed that their bodies and their house had aged together. The effects of the fallen world were magnified in My eyes, while others only saw the brokenness as normal life.

Ima's parents eventually moved in with their eldest son when they needed extra help. Ima's brothers, My uncles, carried the weight of support for their parents. This was the way of our people. It was one of the aspects of the fulfillment of the fifth commandment, the command to honor our fathers and mothers. My parents took this to heart and never grumbled. It was not a decision to be made, just another step of life for all of us.

Time after time, I saw death masquerading as life. It was amazing to see how those of earth dealt with the fallenness of their world as if it were just another sunrise. Destruction, disaster, disease, oppression, and death were common occurrences with little contemplation of anything being different. Adam and Eve were the only inhabitants of earth who knew life before the fall of creation. The fallenness of earth would one day be confronted by the kingdom of God through Me.

Abba was a good man and strong in spirit. He loved God, My Heavenly FATHER, and he loved us. The discipline he exercised in our home was firm but always with love and mercy. Abba was usually quiet and always hard-working. The image of his calloused and sinewy hands, the hands of a carpenter, were etched in My earthly memory. Long after his death, at night before sleep came to My eyes, I often visualized his strong hands at work with wood.

Abba was greatly respected for his work, though it was not fancy. He was a tradesman more than an artist, yet I loved to marvel at his handiwork.

I found it interesting when Abba taught us about God. My heart was warmed when My earthly father taught Me about My Heavenly FATHER. I loved to hear his earthly perspective while knowing the heavenly.

Our house was filled with Abba's creations of tables and carved spoons, just as My FATHER's universe was filled with His creations. I saw the connection of fatherhood, as fathers created an environment for life. Viewing life on earth from the standpoint of the Son of Man, I could see the influence of heaven as the Son of God.

Years rolled by and life changed. I watched Abba's body became worn from the hard labor. He had to cut trees, split them, and hew the wood into boards for the pieces he needed. After all the preparation, then came the actual construction. It was intensive labor from start to finish. He was patient with Me as a boy and young man. Abba taught Me about wood, stone, tools, and life.

Even in early childhood, I puttered around with Abba in his small shop and in the village of Nazareth. When I was older and could help more than being in the way, I went with him to Sepphoris, the city just to the northwest of us.

The city was prosperous and was home to many wealthy people. Fortunately for the people of Nazareth, it was an easy walk to Sepphoris, where much of their work and trade were done. It was the largest city in Galilee, so we were blessed to have a large city nearby to provide work opportunities. We had a dual blessing, as we were also able to enjoy the peace and serenity of a small village like Nazareth.

It would have been difficult for Abba to earn much money in Nazareth, as it was a very small village with only a few hundred people with little money. Our neighbors were mostly shepherds or day laborers. Sepphoris was the source of livelihood in one way or the other for the folks of Nazareth.

As I approached manhood, it was expected of Me to be Abba's apprentice. I was to learn his trade and add My labor to the upkeep of our family. This method of the older teaching the younger was the way of our people and the world. Sons became disciples of their fathers. The slow and steady process of apprenticeship would eventually be the method used with My future disciples.

I was excited to move into manhood. Man was brought forth

to create. Now the One who created trees would cut and carve them. Wood and sometimes stone became the practical focus of My everyday life. Abba and I had to procure trees from the hills and drag them to our shop. Sometimes he would buy lumber in the big city if he had a particular project requiring imported wood. Abba was also skilled as a builder, whether wood or stone. He loved the work of wood more than stone, but it was necessary for him to be competent with both. I became very familiar with the principles of building structures with the use of wood and stone.

Many of the parables in the coming years would be born on the jobsite or from the lives of ordinary people in the villages and towns. Common and uneducated people understood the spiritual principles when they were interwoven with the elements of the familiar world. Sometimes as Abba taught Me his trade, he would also relate our work to our spiritual life. He taught Me more than the work of wood.

One day, we worked to lay a rock foundation of a house we were building. We stopped at noon to eat some grapes and hide from the sun overhead.

During our rest, Abba told Me, "Jesus, when we build a house, it is very important to build a strong foundation. The house must withstand many things, such as storms. If there is no foundation, then the house is built on the ground. The wood will rot, and the house will be weakened. When a big storm of rain and wind comes, surely one day the house will fall with a big crash. And so it is with life. If a man does not form his life on the Word of Adonai, the storms of life will overcome him. He will surely fall into ruin. Do you understand?"

"Yes, Abba! I can see why you remain standing during hard times."

He smiled, rubbing My head. "Oh, I have such a wise son!"

"Perhaps I am wise because I have a wise father," I replied.

He laughed and then looked quite serious as if an overwhelming thought had flooded his mind.

I grew strong in body with the rigorous work of a builder. There was a measure of joy in the hard labor of making something with My own hands out of raw wood. Articles and buildings were usually made of the materials available in our area. Imported materials were only affordable for the rich. We learned to adapt and use what we had.

When Abba began to grow older, more was required of James and Me. We were only about two years apart in age. Our younger brothers began to help just as soon as they were strong enough to work and mature enough to stay out of trouble. Abba did not tolerate foolishness on the job. He was extremely focused while working.

The beginning of a project often began the same way. Abba would choose a tree, make the first cuts, and then turn the ax or saw over to us. Then it was limbed. Our younger brothers made themselves useful by dragging the larger limbs to our home for firewood and chopping them to usable size. Very little was wasted; everything had to count in our survival. Some of the wood only good for the fire was shared with our aging grandparents and older neighbors. We learned to work, and we learned to share.

When the length of logs was chosen, we would tie ropes to the heavier pieces and drag them to our place. Smaller pieces were hoisted onto our shoulders for the journey down the hillsides.

Once, as I bore a log on My shoulder, suddenly I felt a weight heavier than the actual wood. For just a moment, I sensed a future weight of wood that would plummet Me into the dirt. As time went, FATHER often sent glimpses of future events into My senses to deepen the understanding of My destiny. Often they were only moments of a futuristic dream. These dreams or visions were never given to overburden but rather to strengthen Me for the journey ahead.

It was in times like this that I would get whiffs of the future. They were always measured so that My heart would not be overburdened. My human mind and emotions, especially in My youth, did not have the capacity to embrace everything all at once. FATHER gave Me calculated portions to fully establish My purpose without overwhelming My humanity.

The amount of work to turn logs into a table was a long process. First, we debarked the log. Then we split it into boards with an ax, wooden wedges, and a maul. The rough boards were then further smoothed with a draw knife or wood plane.

Abba always supervised our work. When we were just beginning to learn, he started the work, demonstrating the skill, and then allowed us to have a hand in it. When the details became more complicated, he would take the tools from our hands. He was a wonderful teacher, delegating more intricate work to us as our knowledge and skill developed.

Years later, I used the same teaching principles that I learned from Abba. My disciples learned first by observation as I ministered. Then they ministered while I supervised. A disciple was much like an apprentice. When necessary, just like Abba, I would need to intervene with My disciples when they became overwhelmed by a difficult situation.

As time passed, Abba taught Me and James even more of his trade. My arms and hands grew stronger from working with the tools and wood. The skills became second nature with the repetitive work. We built and repaired everything, from wooden bowls to houses. I learned to measure, saw, chisel, carve, and drill. The laying of stone was also a skill I learned. The work was hard but rewarding when we observed the pieces coming together as a whole.

I realized one aspect of Father's image was the creative side. In My eternal past, We had created the world and all that was in it. Man was made in Our image; his creative nature was an aspect of Deity's image. As I watched Abba craft beautiful things from a simple piece of wood, I also witnessed the creative image of God in the work of his hands.

The fallen nature of man was apparent in many of the happenings of our world. We had endowed man with this creative nature, but it was through his fallen spirit that he turned things meant for good into something evil or twisted. It was a warped turn to man's creative mind; he imagined an evil purpose from something intended for good. This corrupted line of thinking ran the entire length of human history.

As Jews, we had witnessed the brutality of the Romans oppressing our people. Some of the soldiers took pleasure in horrific acts of cruelty from which we had no recourse. It took a depraved and evil mind to utilize such things as the crucifixion to strike fear in an occupied people. The Romans were masters of cruelty. I knew that the tyrants of all the ages would use the same principles in newer methods of oppression.

A piece of wood could be carved into a spoon to help feed the hungry or it could be fashioned into a war club to kill another man. This was the contrast of the creative mind: it could be used for good or for evil. I remembered how this grieved the heart of Father to see the very trait of creativeness be corrupted into evil.

One day, a man came with a beautiful piece of cedar wood and wanted Abba to carve an image of an idol. I remember the appalled look on Abba's face, which quickly turned to righteous anger. He scolded the man for having such an evil desire to turn away from the living God to serve a wooden idol.

The man did not relent but tried to flatter him into doing the work. He went on and on about how he admired My father's handiwork. This boiled Abba's outrage even more, and the man had the audacity to tempt him with double payment for the work.

Abba shamed him and told him, "Even if you give me half of all your goods, I will not defile the name of Adonai by creating an adulterous idol by the work of my hands! Take your evil money and your chunk of dead wood and go!" With that, he threw the cedar wood into the street and spit into the dirt to show his disgust.

The man walked away, scoffing under his breath.

My heart leaped for joy at seeing the righteousness of Abba. On the other hand, it crushed My heart to see the blindness of the man with the cedar wood.

I recalled the scripture from the prophet Isaiah, where a foolish man carved and then worshipped a wooden idol. Afterwards he baked his bread from the wood shavings that remained from the sculpture. The evilness of idolatry barely overshadows the blindness of their minds.

The very next day, I was shaping a table leg with a drawknife. While I was shaving the long, curled slivers from the wood, I was bewildered. Why would a man worship a piece of wood? I knew the depravity of a sinful man caused his mind to be futile when it came to worship. It was such a shame that men would worship the created rather than the Creator.

The psalm of King David said it so beautifully: "The heavens declare the glory of God; And the firmament shows His handiwork" (Ps. 19:1). Yes, the wonder of creation declared the glory of God. This was the reason FATHER had sent Me into Our creation, to rescue man from the very sinful creature he had become.

When I became older and more skilled with the work, some people mused about My future as a builder. Some talked about Me taking over the business, as I was the eldest son. A few even praised My work and talked about My future as a carpenter. I just smiled and went about My business as though everything was going as planned. It was going as planned but not as they thought. I had learned from Abba and Ima to keep My thoughts long and My speech short.

FATHER had sent Me to earth with a divine purpose. If that purpose was fully known, some would have questioned the reason I was working as a carpenter. In the plans of FATHER, the purpose and timing were perfect and must not be corrupted. Now was not the appointed time, yet I was still on the path of FATHER's purpose.

There will always be those who have a purpose but whose foolish zeal will cause them to step through the door too soon. They spoil the process and the outcome of God's purpose. Then there are others with a purpose who procrastinate because of their fear or timidity. These wait and the sun sets on God's desire, thus they forfeit their destiny. I knew there was a heavenly purpose for Me; I was only awaiting FATHER's perfect timing and plan.

Now and in My future journey, timing would be of the utmost importance. Some individuals, being impatient or afraid, would urge Me to act prematurely. Other people, when it was important for Me to act, would urge caution or delay. I always had to be sensitive to FATHER's desire and plan.

CHAPTER NINE

FINAL YEARS IN NAZARETH

............ಿಸಿ-ಎ-೧-ಲ್ಲ೫೦ಶ೪೨/೦೦೦-ಇ-ಲ್ಲ............

And Jesus increased in wisdom and stature,
and in favor with God and men.

LUKE 2:52

A bba was older than My mother by ten years. She had only been a teenager when I was brought forth into the world. At the time, he had been well established in his work as a young carpenter and with adequate income for a family. The husband being some years older than his bride was not unusual for our people. Girls, when they developed into womanhood, were considered ready for marriage and childbirth. Men were expected to be able to provide for the livelihood of their young families when they married.

It was one month after we had celebrated the Feast of Tabernacles when Abba began telling us of his terrible headaches. Some days he was fine; other days he could not work. James and I began to take responsibility for the daily work. Our younger brothers were also learning more of the trade and stepped up to share the burden. We pulled together as a family and prayed for Abba while we worked to provide for our family.

One morning, he did not wake from his sleep. Ima cried out to Me at an early hour, "Jesus, come here quick!"

I rushed to his bedside and saw My mother's concerned look before I saw his pale face. I put My ear to his chest and felt relief that he was still breathing, though it was shallow.

My heart broke. Lying before Me was My father. I would become known as the "healing prophet" to the common people, but now I could not go beyond My FATHER's timing.

One day, I would touch paralytics and they would walk. I would apply mud to the eyes of the blind and they would see. I would speak to the dead and they would live, but not today. My heart crumbled within My chest.

Now Abba lay dying before Me, and I was not allowed to heal him. It was his time to die but not My time to heal. This was very difficult for Me. My mind wanted him to live, but in My spirit, I knew FATHER had another purpose for him and for Me.

Ima sent Joses to summon the local physician. The old physician came as soon as his old, stiff legs could carry him. He had a small bag of ointments and herbs. His training was meager, having apprenticed under another physician. In many ways, he was self-taught. If the truth had been known, most of the sick he treated would have naturally recovered without his poultice or herbs. It was understandable that people wanted everything possible to be done to relieve pain or to live, so he was often called but did little.

The old physician listened to Abba's breath, opened his eyelids, and looked into his eyes. He asked Ima several questions. I perceived that beneath his outward look of confidence, he was a caring but helpless man. He went through his motions to appear as if he were doing something to heal, but no healing would come.

He told Ima to cool his fever with a cold, wet rag. From his bag, he pulled a small bag tied with twine; it contained a mixture of powders that had been ground with an apothecary's mortar and pestle. He pinched a measure with his fingers and placed it under Abba's tongue. Abba never flinched or reacted in any way. As his salvia reacted to the powder, it just oozed out the corner of his mouth. Ima wiped it away with a rag.

I noticed the worried look on Ima's face. She was very concerned for the man she loved. He was in the throes of death while she held his hand. Her concern was not only about Joseph but also about the mouths to feed in the coming months and years. In our culture, widowhood was spoken about in the same sense as the poor.

Our beloved physician had done all he knew to do. He looked at Ima with saddened eyes. She was told to keep his fever down with moist cloths and to give him only broth if he woke from his deep sleep. The instructions Ima received were more to keep her busy than to heal. The work of her hands was meant to give her a glimmer of hope, but the experienced physician kept the knowledge of the rattle in Abba's chest to himself. He knew it was only a matter of time before Abba would go the way of all men.

Ima thanked the old physician and placed a few copper coins and a pomegranate into his hands. He graciously accepted them and thanked her. Gathering his wares, he then shuffled helplessly out our door. I watched the old physician amble away. His form was hunched over and covered by his dark and dusty cloak. He had done his best, but it was not enough.

In that moment, I saw the tiredness and helplessness of people with a heart to heal, but in the end, it was just a futile attempt. It was a picture of a fallen world filled with compassionate helpers with little power to bring an end to suffering. I felt the moving in

My spirit. One day I would experience something much different than today's outcome.

This created world had fallen into sin and death, resulting in the eventual dying of all men. Now it was all so personal as I experienced the helplessness of mortal man in the face of death. In My eternal existence, I had seen the death of many millions, but now I was experiencing this as one made of dust.

My heart was shattered. I was seeing the one who had loved Me as his own flesh dying before My eyes. It was heart-wrenching. I sat on a bench at the front of our house, feeling the weight of sorrow. As his son, it felt like My father was leaving too soon, and it hurt very deeply. I wept.

This was the man who took Me as his own, knowing I was not of his stock. There was never a hint from him that I was less than his. He had loved and cared for Me as the rest of his brood. Contrary to the ways of most men, he often treated Me better, knowing who I was. Of all the people alive, none knew better than Ima and Abba that I was virgin-born. And as much as they treated Me as a normal child, they knew I was the Son of God yet to be revealed to the world.

Abba had taught Me to walk. He held My hand as a young boy when we went to the synagogue. We prayed together. We sang the songs of David together. He and I fashioned things of wood together. While we worked side by side, our communication had become one of grunts and nods with seamless understanding.

While thinking about all the wonderful experiences and the life we shared, a torrent of tears streamed down My face. I tried to be brave for Ima, but My soul was moved to grief and My tears unstoppable.

I needed a moment to release My emotions. However, I was the eldest child in the family, and I needed to help Ima and the other children. In My young life, I had witnessed the aftermath of death when many of our neighbors and kindred had died. I knew what was coming in many ways.

Shortly after the physician had exited our home, Ima looked at Me with a question in her glance. Without saying a word, her eyes asked Me, *Can you do anything?* With great sorrow, I shook My head no. Ima knew! It was not My time. She questioned Me no more.

In everyday life, it often appeared that she had forgotten who I really was. We had not talked about it after our big talk, but there was always this understanding between us. She knew something no one else but Abba knew concerning Me. It broke My heart when she looked at Me, holding Joseph's limp hand, and saying with her grieved face, *I know who You are!*

It was not My time. I had visited many people in Nazareth who were sick, carrying them food, water, and firewood. Often, I had helped Abba carry the dead to their tombs. In all these situations, it had never been My time. I knew that one day I would heal the sick, cast out demons, and yes, raise the dead. But today, I could not initiate the power until FATHER said it was time.

Ima put the children to bed as I sat by Abba's bedside. I wiped his face with a dampened cloth and moistened his lips with drops of cool water. It was all I was permitted do.

For a brief visionary moment of only seconds, FATHER gave Me a hint of the future. In My mind's eye, I saw Ima washing blood from My face. Suddenly, I was shaken back to the moment at hand as Ima returned to the bedside and asked, "How is he?"

My only answer was, "He is still the same."

He lived into the night, and sometime past midnight, about the third watch of the night, he breathed his last breath.

For years to come, I would cherish this moment in a strange way. I was with him until the end, and it was a special moment. It was an earthly experience that I now shared with millions of others. This was a life ritual as the living reverently usher their loved ones to eternity. I gave him the last touch of a son's love as he took his last breath. It was a sacred moment.

I cried again when he died. He had been My earthy father. I had spent most of every day of My life in his shadow. We had breathed the same air and walked the same roads. I had learned so much from him. I loved him deeply. He loved me. I was not his child, but he treated Me as the beginning of his strength, his firstborn son.

With his dying, My responsibility as the oldest son greatly changed. I was now the head male in our family. My first duty was to console My mother. I held My widowed mother in a long embrace as she sobbed and cried. I could sense her loss, her fear, and her uncertainty as a widow. I knew I would feel this in the heart of others in the future. As I wiped the tears from her eyes, I softly spoke to her: "Ima, your beloved husband is gone, but do not fear. You have strong sons, and we will care for you."

My heart mourned not only for Abba's death but also for Ima. She had a tender heart, and it was broken. In My more than two decades on this earth, I had witnessed the plight of man. I saw with My eyes, felt with My hands, heard with My ears, and perceived in My spirit the reality of man's condition manifesting itself in oppression, poverty, sickness, and death.

I assisted some of the men in the village to prepare Abba for burial. He was washed, covered with some spices, and wrapped with strips of grave cloths. We carried his body to the burial caves outside of the village for his entombment. Then we observed a week of mourning, with friends coming and going to comfort us. The week ended with a large meal with family, friends, and any who wished to come.

After the days of mourning for Joseph were over, we had to live again. Since I was the oldest, I assumed the position of the family's head. It was now My responsibility to care for, provide for, direct, and protect the family. I was not fearful, for I knew FATHER would provide for us and guide Me in the tasks ahead.

We had a family trade to continue. I had to teach My younger brothers, especially Jude and Simon, the skills and knowledge of a builder. James and Joses were skilled builders with not many years behind Me. My youngest two brothers needed to know about life and be ready to assume the responsibility for our family and their future families.

My brothers did not know, neither would they have understood, that My life would not always be in Nazareth. I had to prepare them for the shift that was coming. This responsibility would be difficult but necessary. I had a lot of work to do before My eventual departure.

And then there was Ima. She was a woman of faith, yet she was scared. Abba had been her rock of stability. She knew that in difficult times, he worked even harder. He always found a way to care for his family at any personal cost or inconvenience. Now he was gone.

I gave Ima more of My time. She always rose before the sun, so I would sit with her while the others slept. I encouraged her and spoke of FATHER's love and care for her. We recited many of the beloved psalms over and over. Mostly, I listened to her. She poured out her heart to Me, voicing her concerns and fears.

After a time of emptying her heart, she would smile and say I was a good listener. These were treasured memories for Me. It was also painful in some ways, knowing she was quite dependent upon Me. My heart ached for the day when I would give her an embrace of departure and walk away.

I knew every person had his or her own story and needed someone with whom to share it. My Ima was no different, and neither were any of the multitude I would encounter on this journey. My ears would hear the stories of many others, and My heart would flow rivers of compassion.

There was a mission in Nazareth for Me to accomplish before My mission to the world. Being the oldest son, I was responsible for establishing and settling the family before My departure. Since James was near My age, I began to groom him for the responsibility ahead. By this time, he was an accomplished carpenter; therefore, it was not that difficult. He and I had almost become like partners even before Abba died.

We had taken much of the load, especially the difficult and strenuous tasks, when Abba became ill. But even when he was unable to do manual tasks, we needed his advice often in our work. Once he was gone, we greatly missed him both in the family and in the family business. He had decades of experience and knew the minute details of his work. He knew such things as how a log would split out by the twist in the wood grain. Much knowledge was buried with him, but he was a wonderful teacher and had shared much of it with his sons.

I had to prepare James to become the head of the family. There was much for My other brothers to learn as well. James and I had to have some firm discussions with them. After Abba died, at first, they slowed their pace with us. I would never be an earthly father, but I received a taste of being a father from the interaction with My younger siblings.

The girls were even more difficult in some ways. They had only known Me as a loving older brother, but now I exerted some fatherlike guidance. Initially, they only giggled, but when they knew I was serious, they quickly got in line with the task at hand.

Adina, the youngest, had the hardest time with the new arrangement. She was quite immature and cried the first time I had to exert some strong fatherly discipline.

Through great sobbing tears, she said, "Jesus, you do not love me anymore. You were so stern with me today. I was just talking with the boy who was visiting our neighbor."

Trying to console her, I said, "Oh, Adina, you know I love you. I was just trying to protect you. The boy you speak of is already a man, and you know nothing about him. I could tell he had bad intentions by the way he was looking at you. Adonai will send you a good husband one day, I am sure. You need to be patient and careful with those you do not know. It is fine to be friendly, but boys think differently than girls."

Her tears had dried, and she smiled, "Yes, dear Brother. I know you meant well. Just let me grow up!"

I laughed. "I cannot stop that! Just look. You are a young woman, not a girl anymore. Maybe I can put a rock on your head to keep you short. Now go fetch some water from the well before Ima makes you cry!" Off she went, giggling.

My sisters were good girls but just crossing the line from girls to women. They were trying to find their place in the world and needed a fatherly perspective on many issues. I had to set their course and made it plain. Yet with all My forced fatherly demeanor, they knew I had a soft place in My heart for their sad eyes. I dreaded the day I would have to kiss their soft cheeks goodbye.

Long before I left Nazareth, I assisted Ima in finding the proper suitors for My sisters. As the oldest son, I assumed the fatherly position in the arrangements of their husbands-to-be. This was more painful for them than Me. On more than one occasion I had to flatly deny a young man of any hopes of marrying one of My sisters. I was sure they had no idea who they were dealing with in the arrangements.

As I began to approach thirty years of age, the destiny of FATHER was drawing Me like the pull of earth to a falling tree. The years of life in a loving home, comforted by the familiar, were quickly becoming uncomfortable in an odd way. It was not that things were bad, but this life I had known on earth for almost thirty years was losing its necessity. I was being drawn to a horizon that was beyond Nazareth.

It was not a mental decision as much as an inner yearning. It was like a deep spiritual fountain within ready to burst into the light of day. This fountain would soon create a wave that would change not only the dynamic of our little family but that would crash into this wicked world with an intensity not yet known.

There was much to do before I left. I had to make sure the carpentry work was secure in My brothers' hands. I had entrusted more and more of the daily work to them. They were getting comfortable with unsupervised work and were doing very well in our trade.

In a real sense, they were My first disciples but of carpentry rather than ministry. I learned much about being a leader of men by leading My younger brothers. The organization of daily activities is a skill you can only learn by watching others and then doing. Life puts us in contact with many different and often difficult people, so the navigation through these many personalities is demanding.

Ima was learning to rely on James for more of the family affairs as well. I had delegated some of the household decisions to him, and Ima was very confident in his knowledge and wisdom. He would take the lead in our family when I left. Widows of our people were very dependent upon their sons, especially the older ones.

James had really developed as a man. He was quite serious, sometimes too serious. I was learning as a man of earth that everyone's strength also has an element of weakness. Our younger brothers were good workers, but they were also good-natured pranksters. James had no appetite for folly, but he was learning to bear with it to a degree. He had to learn that his furious overreaction was the very motivation for his fun-loving brothers' tricks. They loved to see his face red and eyes wide.

Given the ways of all My brothers, it was necessary for Me to temper their relationships in our work and family. I had private conversations with each of them and over time molded them into a good working unit. James even began to laugh at himself after a little friction turned to smiles and backslapping laughs. I taught My brothers not only about carpentry but also about working together and our faith.

My brothers began to enjoy some of the responsibility that once rested on My shoulders. Joses particularly liked it when I referred his table work to a prospective customer. And Jude had a unique method of fashioning cartwheels. It was really satisfying to see My brothers becoming independent of Me.

James had married a wonderful young lady who also helped to soften some of his hard edges. Then Joses's wedding was just two years after James's marriage. It was important that My siblings were making their way in life. They all knew of their continuing responsibility to take care of our widowed mother. It was the way of our people, and most men were faithful to it. My brothers were no exception and never wavered from their responsibility.

Several of My sisters were also married. I made sure their husbands were good men. They were beginning to make a full life for themselves with children and homes. They all lived in Nazareth and were present almost daily in our lives. Ima enjoyed the added blessing of being a grandmother to the little ones, which gave her much solace after Abba's death.

Uncle was a new role for Me as well. I loved the young ones in our growing family. It pained Me that My earthly relationships were about to change in a drastic way. I knew the sacrifice of being obedient to FATHER would take on many forms.

I still climbed the little hill where I was awakened to My Messiahship. Time with My FATHER had steadily increased into My adulthood. My spiritual life was taking more of My time. Work, with My brothers, was steadily decreasing.

My brothers seemed to be a little annoyed at first with My frequent absence as I handed more of the carpentry work over to them in preparation for My eventual departure from Nazareth. They never openly called Me lazy, but a few slight words indicated their frustration. But My strong-willed brothers were not going to sway Me from My purpose. I continued to help with the work while in Nazareth, but My daily priorities were quickly changing.

Even though they did not totally understand, they could sense something was coming to a point. A point they neither knew nor would understand.

CHAPTER TEN

BAPTISM IN THE JORDAN

⸺⸺⸺⸺

This is My beloved Son, in whom I am well pleased.

MATTHEW 3:17

As the time for My leaving Nazareth came closer, My first discussion with anyone was with Ima. One convenient day, when everyone was gone from our home, I talked with her about My approaching departure.

The conversation began with, "Ima, you know someday soon I will be leaving Nazareth. I must follow FATHER's will and purpose. I know it will not be easy for any of us, but it is necessary that I go."

With a sad face and forced smile, she replied, "Yes, I knew this day would come. I know it is something You must do. You will do great things, just as I was told before You were conceived. It will not be easy because I know in life the good often comes with difficulties."

I agreed, "Yes, Ima. This is very true!"

She continued with a distant look in her eyes as she remembered: "When You were a child, with the cares of life, I would momentarily forget the prophesies about You. Perhaps it was because I wanted to savor the moments of Your childhood unhindered by spoken words of prophets and angels. The one that causes me the most grief in quiet moments is Simeon's word when he said, 'a Sword will pierce through your soul also.'" (Luke 2:35).

She added, "I still do not know exactly what that means, but I know it will be grievous when it comes. I know I must trust Adonai."

We smiled together as we often did in these moments. My only reply was, "Yes, Ima. That is always the thing we must do, trust FATHER."

She then returned to our discussion by asking, "When will you be leaving?"

"By the end of next month. I will be sure everything is ready for you all here. There is never a good time, but there is only the right time. I must be obedient as I told you when I was twelve: 'I must be about My FATHER's business'" (Luke 2:49).

I gripped her hand. "He is leading Me from here."

We both had a little laugh as we recalled the temple reunion when they realized I was missing for several days.

Ima looked into My face and with moist eyes told Me, "Oh, Jesus, even now when you speak, I hear the wisdom of God in Your voice. Your words touch My heart so deep. I know others from our own synagogue and village talk of the great strength in Your words."

The discussion with My brothers did not go as well. They did not understand why I would leave them with all the work that needed to be done. It was unexplainable to them. It was difficult to describe a heavenly calling to those entwined by earthly endeavors. My future disciples would feel the same pain, but I felt it first. It was not easy leaving a conversation unfinished, with questions unanswered to the satisfaction of the hearers. Eyes covered with the scales of this world do not see the light of heaven.

When My time came to leave, no one really understood except Ima. She always knew that this day and other days were to come. Alone with Me, she recalled some of the events at My birth and infant years. These things were never spoken with My siblings' ears nearby. At the time of her offering of purification after My birth, an old man named Simeon foretold of My mother's heartbreak related to My revelation to the world and the ultimate sacrifice of her Son.

My brothers begrudged My leaving because they knew the full workload would be upon them. They would not understand the importance of all this until several years later. My sisters were saddened about My leaving and were confused why our lives could not continue as they had been. I had become a replacement father to them since Abba's death.

Our extended family, especially My uncles and older cousins, questioned Me about where I was going and what I was going to do. They quizzed Me about marriage, work, and where I would live. Those conversations were very frustrating because they did not understand My purpose on earth. I was limited with what I could explain, so much was left unsaid.

My explanation was veiled to the point that they were more confused after our conversations than before. I left many conversations with the hearers shaking their heads in confusion. For the unseeing of God's plan, it is difficult to hear and perceive the truth.

Some months before, news had reached Nazareth about our near kinsman John, the son of Zacharias and Elizabeth. He was preaching and baptizing on the eastern side of the Jordan River across from Jericho. His ministry was very prophetic, calling for people to repent of their sins and be baptized. Some heard he was like a madman, declaring men to be evil like snakes and in need of a thorough ceremonial cleansing by baptism to wash away their sins. Others questioned if he was the Messiah.

At the first mention of John's preaching, My spirit was greatly quickened. All the village gossip concerning John did not persuade Me, for I knew who he was. There would be no greater prophet than him. Those who refused him or mocked him would be as starving dogs refusing bread.

While making My final preparations to leave Nazareth, I only told My questioners that I was going to see John first. Immediately many thought I was leaving to be one of his disciples. Several mocked Me for seeking after a mad prophet who wore coarse robes and lived in the wilderness. This talk brought laughter to a few. A man with a call and a purpose is often ridiculed. The chosen of God are often the scorned of men.

Knowing that further explanations would not bring understanding to their minds, I said little else to them. I simply told them My mission was beyond the baptizer's work. This brought more confusion to their clouded minds and critical spirits. I was getting accustomed to strange looks and laughing jeers. There was more to say, but this was all they needed for now.

My brothers received a few final instructions from Me the day before I departed. On the day of My parting, I hugged My brothers, kissed My sisters farewell, and gave Ima a long embrace. I walked away without looking back and sensed their eyes on My back. I turned hard right down another road out of sight, knowing that from this point forward, life would never be the same for them, Me, or the world.

The journey from Nazareth to the Jordan River was made with much reflection. My mind witnessed again the experiences of My childhood when I first came to the messianic awareness. The experience of first knowing the truth of who I was and the consciousness of it all was exhilarating to My human emotions.

The importance of My purpose lessened the pain of My leaving, the coming rejection, and the eventual suffering. My steps were intentional and filled with great expectation for the journey of fulfillment that was underway.

My journey through the small villages and towns caused no stir because to them I was just another pilgrim on a journey. They had little idea of where I came from or where My journey would end. Father had desired this, that I would look common to the eyes of men. For this segment of the journey, My obscurity was a blessing. For now, I was happy to gather My thoughts and pray as I walked. And so, I journeyed as any other man, but My path of destiny was like no other's. The ordered steps I took were like nothing before or anything after.

I traveled from Nazareth down through the Jezreel Valley along a route like the one we had traveled on the yearly pilgrimages to Jerusalem. The first part of this trek was also the course Abba and Ima had made on their trip to Bethlehem some thirty years ago. I thought of how hard it must have been for her, being so great with child, to make this trip. She made that fateful journey not only for the purpose of a tyrant's tax but also for the fulfillment of a prophesy for My life.

I was traveling loosely attached to a small caravan. My people often did this for safety along the way. It was difficult for robbers to distinguish a lone traveler from a straggler behind the others. It would be a ploy I would use in the future, blending into a crowd to hide from those with ill intent.

With this route, our little caravan would journey through Samaria. These poor Samaritans were despised by My people because of the long-held animosity and their wayward religious beliefs. They insisted that Mount Gerizim should be the center of worship instead of Jerusalem. When a caravan traveled south during the times of our feast, it was not unusual for us to be jeered occasionally by a Samaritan. The only scrolls they read were those of Moses; they ignored the others altogether. We spent little time in the region of the Samaritans. I would return here on a later mission, but for now I was headed to the Jordan River.

Moving farther south, I veered from the route to Jerusalem while bidding My fellow travelers goodbye. I headed east to the fords of the Jordan. When I was a half day's travel from the Jordan, I began to hear chatter on the road of this wild man dressed in camel hair and a leather belt. There were mixed opinions about him, which was no surprise to Me. He was a true prophet; people either loved him or hated him, with the latter being the majority.

Everyone had an opinion of John, but only a few followed him. Such was the life of a prophet. It seemed that the religious leaders either held him in contempt or were skeptical, but the common people flocked to hear him and be baptized.

After leaving the caravan, I continued traveling east through Jericho. I forded the Jordan River at the usual crossing at the border of the regions of Perea and Judah. The ford was close to the place where John was baptizing, so I made My way to see My kinsman the prophet. Traveling down a narrow road that led to the Jordan, I could hear a loud voice some distance away. Because of the distance, I could not distinguish his words, but I felt his spirit.

When I topped the crest of a small hill, I saw a crowd had gathered to hear the fearless prophet of God. They were people from all stations of life. I knew from their reactions that they were either enthralled or appalled by his words. Some shouted approval of his message while others jeered. John was a true prophet; he was not flattered by the affirming few or intimidated by the critics. He was bold as a lion to the skeptics but gentle with the humble and weak.

John the Baptizer was such a sight. His overall appearance

showed that he took no interest in other people's opinions. He was oddly clothed in a coarse camel-hair tunic with a leather strap tied around his waist. His hair was long and unkempt, and his beard looked as if it had never known a comb. He looked the very part of a wild-eyed prophet standing on the shore. The glory of God was on his face while the tangle of travel was in his hair.

His voice penetrated the atmosphere with a boom. He was loud and brash, with a hint of hoarseness from his frequent loud preaching. His message this afternoon was peppered with, "Repent and be baptized for the removal of your sins!" He would spew a list of sins and scold his listeners to "Flee from the coming wrath of God and repent, you sinners!"

I stood to one side, listening to his words and watching the crowd. My spirit stirred within Me. Israel had not heard a notable prophet in four centuries. But now, on the bank of the river stood the greatest, and all could hear when his voice thundered. It was a magnificent sight to behold. The crowd was transfixed on the prophet, and the prophet was transfixed on God!

I knew John mostly as a boy. The picture in My mind was still vivid of when we sat at the Passover meal, gazing at the cup of wine set for the prophet Elijah. He was now a full-grown prophet, walking in the steps of Elijah, though wine had never touched his lips. He was a great man of God who gripped the hearts of the common people and rattled the brains of the leaders. When his voice thundered, men's hearts trembled.

He gathered up the edges of his robe, tucked them into the leather belt, and waded into the waters of the Jorden. When the waters were to his waist, he turned back toward the shore. He bellowed like a strong bull, "Repent and be baptized for the remission of your sins."

One by one, members of the crowd stepped into the water.

John took them under and raised them up again. He told the baptized ones to go and bear fruit of their repentance from sin.

At first, the repentant disciples were just a few, but they inspired a crowd who then funneled into the water. As the numbers lessened to a dribble, I saw the remaining ones on shore nervously showing their awkwardness over unrepentant sins.

When those seeking baptism ceased, one of the wet disciples cried out in exuberance to John, "Are you the Messiah?"

He answered, "No. As I have told you before, I am not the Messiah. I go before Him to declare His coming."

One from the crowd yelled, "There is no greater prophet than you!"

John shook his head. "I indeed baptize you with water unto repentance, but He who is coming after me is mightier than I, whose sandals I am not worthy to carry. He will baptize you with the Holy Spirit and fire" (Matt. 3:11).

Before John came out of the water, he made one last appeal: "Anyone else who desires to baptized?"

I knew it was My time. I had been standing aside under the shade of a small tree, and I began My steps to the water. When I stepped into it, John's eyes locked upon Mine in wonder and amazement. He had known Me before as a kinsman, but I perceived by his eyes that he knew I was the Messiah.

When I reached John and put My hand on his arm, I realized he was shaking. The bold preacher, now with a humble and soft voice, spoke to Me: "You come to baptized by me? I need You to baptize me!"

I simply replied, "It is fitting and needful for Me to fulfill all righteous requirements of God and man."

John did not completely comprehend My words, but he understood by the Spirit and complied with My request. With tears in his eyes and a quiver in his voice, he declared, "I baptize

You to fulfill all righteousness!" With trembling hands, he placed Me under the water. In those few moments of earthly time, an eternity flowed past Me with the stream of the Jordan's water. From before creation to the present flowed the destiny of FATHER through the ages. All that had transpired before in the life of man on the earth was washed to the past, and a new future of power was about to be born.

When My face crashed through the surface of the water, I opened My eyes to see a magnificent sight. I saw the skies parted to reveal heaven with Holy Spirit descending upon Me as a dove, inhabiting His reclaimed roost on the Son. The dynamic of the Triune was rejoined as FATHER declared from heaven, "This is My beloved Son, in whom I am well pleased" (Matt. 3:17). FATHER, Son, and Spirit in unison as before, except the Son of God was tabernacling among men as the Son of Man.

The invigorating power of Holy Spirit surged through My entire being. Since My messianic awareness, I had much more understanding and many moments of clarity of purpose, but this was even more. The once-budding Son of dust was now in full bloom as the Son of glory.

FATHER had purposed for Me to come as a man. My spirit, as the Son of God, was eternal, but My physical man was finite. My body had a beginning in the womb of My mother; therefore, it was subject to the difficulties of man. My eternal spirit was infinite, pure, and powerful. My earthly tent would become cold, tired, and hungry. I knew the power of Deity. However, in this dimension of earthly existence, I would also know the frailties of the human state.

Now at the beginning of My revelation to the world, I was rejoined by Holy Spirit to empower Me. This empowerment as the Son of Man by Holy Spirit would be a demonstrative model of those who would follow in My steps. My coming to earth was heaven's invasion of this fallen world to redeem man and creation from sin and death.

After My baptism and with Holy Spirit remaining on Me, I was flushed with greater power and wonder. It was so invigorating that I pulled away from the crowd until a more settled calm filled My soul.

I needed to talk with John, but I could not linger for more than a night. Even now the sun was beginning to dip toward the western horizon. Those on the riverbank began to peel away to their homes as the day bid farewell to the light.

Soon the only ones with Me on the riverbank were John and his disciples. John told his disciples that he and I needed to talk alone. His disciples scurried about, making a fire and cooking some locust beans from the carob tree in a pot.

We moved away from the others to sit under a large shrub tree. John began, "Jesus, at first I did not recognize You as My kindred, but I immediately knew You were the Coming One. My spirit leapt within me when I saw You on the upper bank of the river.

"When You came into the water, my heart was pounding in my chest. You were the reason I was sent forth to prepare the way. I am the voice in the wilderness declaring Messiah's coming. My heart is close to bursting even now. You are the Messiah! Praise Adonai! I have longed for this day!"

He continued as tears flowed down his cheeks, "After your baptism, I was amazed at the Spirit descending and staying upon You. When the thunderous voice from heaven confirmed all I knew, it was more than my mind and heart could contain. Now I can die. My purpose has been fulfilled on the earth."

I told John he still had work to do. Only our FATHER would determine his days and the completion of his mission.

John wanted to know if I was going to continue with him, because he wanted so much to be with Me. He knew I was to increase and he was to decrease, all in the timing of FATHER. It made Me sad to tell him no, that I had a journey that was not ours to share. I would be leaving the next morning, but I planned to see him again on My return through this region.

We joined the others around the fire. They offered Me a bowl of vegetable broth, but I declined the offer. These men were used to regular fasting, so they knew My reason for not eating.

The conversation with John turned to our common family. We talked about the times in our youth when we shared festivals and family visits. For a few hours, it was like old times, but a new world was about to erupt in our lives. The purpose of FATHER disrupts the usual lives of men. God's destiny now flowed through our spirits like our blood flowed through our veins.

When I laid on My mat by the dying fire, a fire blazed in My soul. It was difficult to fade into sleep as thoughts and emotions coursed through My mind and heart. In My sleep, the dreams were not vivid, but there was a whirl of flowing colors and powerful winds that reminded Me of a time before My conception.

I awoke early in the morning before the sun rose. I found a secluded place behind a clump of shrub trees and prayed to FATHER. He was preparing Me for the many days ahead. My communion with FATHER and Spirit this morning was beyond the soil upon which I knelt. I knew the forty days ahead to the south would be exhilarating and challenging. This morning was the priming point.

I returned to the sleeping prophet and roused him before the others woke. I told him farewell and that I planned to see him in less than two months. John looked at Me as if he were trying to say something that he could not articulate. I saw the moisture in his eyes as being that of one enraptured by emotions with no words to speak. We embraced, and he kissed My face. I walked away while his hungered gaze followed Me until I was out of sight.

Now the Spirit was urging Me back across the Jordan to the western side. Once in Jericho, I journeyed south, heading to the Judean wilderness. I did not stop to talk with anyone and took My journey in solitude. I had a future destiny leading Me to an immediate destination—the wilderness desert.

I eventually stepped into the vast desert of the Judean wilderness, where there were no villages or people within a day's journey. At the river's edge, I had been surrounded by people and the prophet. Now it was silence, except for an occasional bird and the wind.

CHAPTER ELEVEN

DESERT WILDERNESS

*Then Jesus, being filled with the Holy Spirit, returned from
the Jordan and was led by the Spirit into the wilderness.*

LUKE 4:1

The urge to leave the crowd and be immersed in the
solitude of the desert wilderness with FATHER and Spirit
was overwhelming. I moved into the desert with a desire
as intense as a wandering man seeking water in the foreboding
landscape. So appropriate was the desert, for I was thirsting
for solitude with FATHER. I would not eat or drink for forty
days, which would cause My concentration to be focused on the
spiritual, not the carnal.

It was a relief to be beyond the noise of people and bustling
of roads. Now all I could hear was the current of the wind from
the southwest and the *Breath of the Spirit*.

Leaving the road behind and going into the pathless desert
wilderness was like entering another world in some ways. The
absence of people was an environment only those seeking solitude
could easily enjoy. My life had been filled with people, and in
the months ahead crowds would gather around Me. For now,

this desert was My home, and solitude was My oasis. My only companions were Father and Holy Spirit. I also knew the adversary was lurking behind the bushes, awaiting an opportunity to hinder and destroy.

The sun had set in the west. A bit of reddish orange still hung on the horizon. I had traveled some distance into the desert at this point, gathering a few sticks and bits of tinder for a fire as I walked. With My flint and iron, I sparked a fire in the tinder and then added small sticks to nurture the flame. Next, I added a few larger sticks to warm Me from the night air. The fire gave Me some comfort as I reclined after My long day. I began to pray to Father.

"Oh Father! The wonder of Your power and wisdom fills My mind. My spirit within Me feels the flood of spiritual waves that cannot be contained in the reservoir of My human soul."

My consciousness became dreamy, and I floated from the sounds of the desert night to the wafts of the Spirit. I was caught between two worlds, feeling the warmth of the fire and the fire of Holy Spirit. I felt a surge of the same power that held the universe in order. It was as if My body was floating on a sea of spiritual billows, causing Me to rise and fall with every wave. My physical body was exhausted. I drifted into peaceful sleep and dreams of eternal glory and wonder.

When I awoke, just a few embers remained of My fire. The sun had cracked the eastern horizon and gave the promise of more heat than needed. But for now, the cool chill of the early desert morning was My greeting for a new day.

A short distance away, some shrubs formed a natural canopy of protection from the coming heat. I made the short walk and settled My knapsack on a limb. I climbed onto a nearby boulder to witness the rising of the sun—a glorious succession of yellow, red, and finally, blazing orange.

The rising sun was like My earthly life with FATHER. When I was a child, He was first a glimmer of eternity; later He was a glory that overpowered My human senses. It is an exhilaration understood only in the spiritual realm, but it overwhelmed the natural man.

I sat unhurried with no plan or agenda. Here on this rock, in this desert, I was laying My life as a canvas before the One who in His wisdom brought vivid colors to life. I prayed with words: "Blessed are You, My FATHER, the Maker of heaven and earth. How wondrous are Your ways. Your mercies are sure, and Your wisdom is beyond measure." After some time of praying, words were no longer needed. I felt His embrace and the whisper of His voice as only a Son understood with no translation. It was more glorious than the sun.

I felt a deepening in My soul and spirit; I eternally knew what was happening. I was in the school of the desert, and FATHER was transferring His strength, wisdom, power, and understanding into My earthly being with greater intensity. He was further empowering Me for My journey of ministry. I knew I was God, the Son in flesh, but this was the course I had to travel. I was in this finite body but from beyond it in the stratospheres of eternity.

After some time, I left My perch on the rock and strolled around the area I had come to sojourn. It had been a day since I had eaten, but the spiritual bread from FATHER sustained Me more than the bread from My mother's hearth. In this spiritual solitude, a fast from food was a necessity.

Here in the desert, the bustling world seemed to stand still. As I communed with FATHER and Spirit, eternity took the place of time. Realms of wisdom and power were imparted to Me in a few moments of time. Day by day, My physical strength became weak from no food, but My spirit and soul became stronger and stronger. I could feel the rush of eternity and the slipping away of earthly focus.

Words of men would surely fail to convey the eternal moments of total absorption into the sphere of the spiritual realm. Many things I knew from eternity as the Son of God were imparted again into the Son of Man. I was the One destined from beyond ages and the only true heir to the throne. I was always meant to be, and now I was. And so, it was with Me; I was the King anointed from eternity by FATHER to walk this road of redemption and one day fill the throne in His time.

The perspective of the kingdom of God now loomed forever in My consciousness. I could plainly see the deadness and fallenness of the world. Sin, rebellion, and destruction had wrecked the world that was originally created perfect.

Men ambled through life from birth, witnessing the wretchedness of sickness, poverty, disaster, and wickedness as common as a blade of grass. Their experience in this fallen state dimmed the consciousness of their souls to the death and destruction constantly around them. Men saw a filthy leper on the street and saw it as normal. The procession of mourners carrying an old man to his burial was the expected end of all who breathed. It was man's known state of the world, and so they trod down the roads of earth blind, lost, and dying.

FATHER renewed the knowledge of Our original plan and His desire to see man and creation whole. I saw with greater clarity and vision the kingdom of God in My hands, confronting the deadness with the Life of God in full strength. My message would be the kingdom of God bursting into the darkness and deadness of this world. The kingdom was at hand.

The plan of God was opened as a gift of layers. Dead men would receive eternal life by the death of the Son. The Son's resurrection would confirm everlasting life to those who believed in His name. The living sons of God would be resurrected in His likeness to life with no end. Life would be the gift imparted at the paid expense of God Himself in His Son.

My beloved disciple would share this revelation of the scroll sealed with seven seals. No one was found worthy to open the scroll and loosen its seals but the Lion of the tribe of Judah. I was about to roar. The scroll was the everlasting plan of redemption, unveiled by the only One worthy to open its seals. I, the everlasting I AM, the One found worthy to open the seals, bringing redemption for fallen man and creation.

Moments became days, and days became weeks. My time in the desert with FATHER and Spirit was marching to an end. It was a like a pendulum. One moment it was ecstatic joy, and then there were moments of pure horror when the sacrifice of redemption was portrayed. Oh the joy of redemption; oh the horror of the means.

My forty days were approaching their completion, and the plan had been revealed. The adversary knew the gravity of the moment, yet his understanding was skewed and limited. In another dimension of eternity, I remember his adoring eyes of praise as his vocal pipes worshipped the God of all creation. Then his name was Lucifer, the morning star, but his rebellion forced his identity to be conformed to his corrupted nature. He forfeited the identity of glory and took upon himself the position of adversary and the cursed name of Satan.

I also remember his raging eyes when he dared to disrupt eternity and rebelled against God. The glory and peace of heaven were marred for a moment in his rebellion and then relieved at his expulsion. An angelic third who followed his deceitful rebellion were banished as well.

He had learned over the centuries to attack the Creator through the marring of His creation. And he had learned to attack man at his two most vulnerable points: his lowest and his highest. These were the point of want versus abundance, the point of failure versus success, the point of weakness versus power.

Years beyond now, this time in the desert would be described as My time of temptation. In many ways it was, yet also it was a time of solitude with Father and wonderful waves of Holy Spirit revelation. During this time, Satan took advantage of My solitude and bodily weakness by attacking My mind and emotions. He continually attacked and buffeted Me throughout the forty days, but he reserved his most brutal attack for the end.

Being alone in the wilderness of sand with Father and Spirit was wonderful, but with the attacks of the enemy, it was also intense. Satan struck in moments of weak physical strength and emotional exhaustion. He used every ploy to distract and harass My spiritual preparation for the ministry of the days ahead.

The spiritual experience was wave after wave of glory and power up to the very limits of My human tolerance. It was exhilarating and at the same time exhausting. With no physical nourishment, My body trembled under the terrific weight of glory. My flesh crashed as My spirit soared. Then Satan would attempt to counter the move of the Spirit.

The accelerated time of eternal wonder with Father waned to time and space once more. I descended to earthly reality, and My feet felt more of clay again. After these many days of glorious impartation, when I was at My greatest spiritual high, the enemy came with his greatest attack to the place of My weakest flesh. He saw My highest and My lowest states as double targets for his deceptive ploys.

After days of My initial time in the desert, My body had become accustomed to no food. The spiritual ecstasy had overpowered the call of the flesh. When I came down from the spiritual mountain to the valley of flesh, My greatest temptations began. Satan made no orders to his lieutenants for these attacks. He girded himself for direct conflict with the True Heir to the Throne.

As I journeyed in the desert, the most beautiful stones were in My path. They had been rounded by wind and sand and greatly resembled loaves cooked in an earthen oven. They were golden brown like the crust of newly baked bread. Satan whispered his alluring words, "If you are the Son of God, command that these stones become bread" (Matt. 4:3).

I knew I was the Son of God. There was no "if." His spear against the flesh of man was the "if" to induce doubt in God's Word. It was his favorite weapon; he had even wielded it against Eve. I could erase his deceptive doubt with one word, as I, the eternal I Am, was the Word.

The thought of those stones as bread returned. I could taste the soft inside morsel. I could hear the crunch of the golden-brown crust. I could even smell the mouthwatering aroma of freshly baked hot bread.

"What? No!" I saw his deceptive lure clearly. Holy Spirit within My spirit urged forth the truth of the Holy Word. From My lips poured the content of My spirit in full authority: "It is written, 'Man shall not live by bread alone, but by every word that proceeds from the mouth of God'" (Matt. 4:4).

Satan reeled back at the power of the Word of God. He quickly retreated a short distance to regain his composure. I could see in his eyes the hidden hate and could hear the whirl of his wicked mind as he formed his next attack.

Then in a blaze of deceptive power, he immediately transported Me to Jerusalem, to the highest pinnacle of the temple. Here, perched among the heights of this holy house, his deceptive and accommodating voice tried to force the issue with God's Word.

"If You are the Son of God, throw Yourself down. For it is

written: 'He shall give His angels charge over you,' and, 'In their hands they shall bear you up, Lest you dash your foot against a stone'" (Matt. 4:6).

The lure of proving Myself to Satan and the world was real. I could feel the pull of pride to silence the critics and to exalt Myself before FATHER's time. My righteous spirit rose within Me. How dare this prince of demons and the father of lies use the Holy Word in a twist of the truth to form a lie! The strength of the carnal flesh was real, but the power of the Spirit within Me triumphed over his wicked desire.

From the depths of My spirit came this raging truth to dispel the darkness of his lie masquerading as truth. "It is written again, 'You shall not tempt the LORD your God'" (Matt. 4:7).

Knowing that his second attempt was doomed, the master of all deceit moved Me from the temple to a high mountain. Through his power of deception and cunning use of the eye, the deceiver of all deceptions showed Me all the great kingdoms of the world. I saw past the tall buildings of marble and inlaid gold and gazed into the hearts and minds of men with power.

I saw the earthly strategy of dominion, power, and control. Wealth, luxury, fame, and opulence were only the fluff of their deep desire. The overpowering desire of the elites and tyrants of this world was the dominion over lands, the power over people, and the control of the levers of riches and resources. Pride, control, and the love of riches were the heart of world dominion. The blindness of the world hid the true riches of love, humility, compassion, peace, and Godly purpose. Just as gems were hidden beneath the surface, so were the treasures of God concealed in the meek of the earth.

This enemy of God was willing to share a portion of his rule with those who would bolster his ultimate control and gain for him the worship of the world. I felt this pull in his temptation, the desire for power and control.

Springing forth in My consciousness was a crystal-clear ocean of truth that immediately washed away the filth of his stagnant puddle of lies. I knew FATHER's eventual plan, but more importantly, I knew at whose feet all worship was to be laid: the eternal and all-powerful living God, the Creator of all things and everyone!

Satan's third temptation was at first enticing but then sickening. My holy anger rose, and I used the *Sword of the Spirit* against this diabolical tempter: "Away with you, Satan! For it is written, 'You shall worship the LORD your God, and Him only you shall serve'" (Matt. 4:10).

He cowered and fell backward at the rebuke of the Word in My breath. He crawled away like a wounded dog, slinking away with an occasional turned head to see if his attacker would pursue. One day he would be finally banished, but this was not it.

Satan had offered a false, temporary dominion that in the future would be Mine forever. It was a clever attack but ill-informed. One day, I would be the stone cut out of the mountain as in Daniel's prophesy, crushing all these propped-up kingdoms of the world into powder. My kingdom would be an everlasting kingdom, not to be preempted by this false trick of power.

In the history of the world, tyrants would rise and tyrants would fall, but a promised sunrise would come when all the kingdoms of this world became "the kingdoms of the LORD and of His Christ" (Rev. 11:15). I would reign forever. The *Meek One* and his meek ones would inherit the earth.

The spiritual exhilaration of the battle made Me forget the weakness of My flesh for a moment. But soon it returned. I was drained of all human strength. Satan was gone for a season, but so was My physical vigor. I sat on a nearby rock, exhausted and emotionally spent. I knew I had a journey before Me, but now one step seemed like a Sabbath's day journey.

I felt the presence of heavenly messengers before they came into view. Suddenly, a company of angels with brilliant countenances surrounded Me. Eternal remembrance rushed to My mind as I recognized each angel by name. They encircled Me in a ring of protection and comfort. Each girded with a sword, they stood strong and regal. Some were ministering angels of comfort, and others were mighty warriors from near the throne of God.

Every other one was facing inward with their head alert but bowed in holy reverence. The others faced outward with their hands on the hilts of their swords, ready to unsheathe them for any battle or foe.

Some distance beyond, I could see a secondary ring of angelic protectors facing the distance with swords drawn and raised in clasped hands. Then I saw that the surrounding horizon was filled with a multitude of angels mounted on white steeds that pawed at the dust. This army of heaven stood ready and able to destroy all the armies ever mustered and annihilate all the earthly kingdoms ever seated in power. They only awaited one word yet to be commanded.

Then as if on cue, the inner ring parted, and an angel of taller stature walked through their band. He carried a vessel filled with rich broth, a loaf of bread, a jug of milk, one small jar of honey, and a skin of cool crystal-clear water. The meal was offered with an outstretched hand and a bowed head. It was the most nourishing meal as I dipped the bread into the broth and then raised it to My mouth. I sensed My strength renewed and My body replenished. When I drank the heavenly water, the cool stream refreshed My parched throat.

I slowly ate some of the portion and waited, not wanting to overwhelm My weakened body. While I waited, I absorbed the comfort, reverence, and power of this angelic host. Their very presence imparted strength and courage.

After time had passed, the serving angel spoke. "Please eat again, my LORD, for Your journey is before You, and Your FATHER has Your purpose to fulfill."

I ate some more food, drank the milk, and sopped the bread in the honey. I returned the vessels to the angel at My side. Suddenly, I heard swords drawn in a unison salute and heels snapped to attention. Then the angels vanished as quickly as they had come.

The desert around Me was amazingly quiet. Every creature had fled in reverence. A cool breeze brushed My face in the wake of the angels' flight. In the distance, I heard thunder as the angels breached the atmosphere, but not a cloud was in sight.

I was alone again. The only motion was a gentle wind from the west. It was exceptionally quiet compared to the happenings just past. The tenseness of Satan's temptation and the exhilaration of the angelic force were gone. It was as if nothing had transpired, judging by the lonely appearance of this Judean desert.

My physical strength was renewed, and the long walk to Galilee would be a welcome reprieve from My stay in the desert. Here the desert was not as hot as the Negev farther south. There were more islands of shrubs and small tree oases here, bringing a welcome relief from the blistering sun. I moved from My perch on the rock to a nearby oasis to consider My exit from the wilderness.

The shade was a blessing compared to the sun-scorched sand. A small clear spring trickled from under a large boulder. The water formed a small pool that then emptied out into a small stream flowing inward until it was consumed by the sandy soil of the oasis. I drank deeply from the pool and felt the sweet dribble of water from My beard.

I removed My garments and splashed the cool waters on My

hot, dusty body. The cool water washed the dried sweat away, and the breeze left Me feeling refreshed and renewed. It momentarily reminded Me of My baptism in the Jordan and the *Wind of the Spirit* saturating Me on the bank.

I washed My clothes in the small stream, reserving the freshness of the pool for a later drink. I hung My garments on a limb of a small tree at the southern edge of the oasis to dry in the heat of the day. Then, resting on a patch of soft grass, I drifted off into a brief slumber as I contemplated My next step.

As I slept, I dreamed. In the mist of the dream, I was walking through the market of a small town. The air was filled with the common smell of ripe fruits and the refuse of donkeys. There was the usual bustle of a marketplace and busy streets. I sensed men walking close behind Me, gathering in number as we went. Some of their faces came into view, and all but a few were not stately men of wealth or position but common men of Israel. Their faces showed an uncertainty of where they were going, though I could sense their hearts were loyal and their spirits strong.

These men were discounted by others but chosen by FATHER. Oh, the paradox of Our kingdom, where the weak became the strong and the names of obscure men were spoken on the lips of future generation. Volumes would be written about their exploits.

Generations later, even those of My kingdom living out their lives in the dark corners of the world would be heralded in eternity as the great ones.

A gust of wind woke Me from My brief sleep. I rose and peered into the sky to see the position of the sun. It was about five hours from darkness. My clothes were only slightly damp but would dry before the cool of the night.

And now toward Galilee I had to go. Holy Spirit was urging Me on to the next portion of My journey. My soul was excited for this next step, moving out of this wilderness and into the plan of My FATHER.

One night of rest here in the oasis would be nice, but I was ready to be gone from the desert. I gathered My few things, found an adequate stick for a staff, and began My journey toward Galilee.

As I traveled north, I recounted My time in the land behind Me. The time and experience with FATHER and Holy Spirit in the wilderness had been nothing short of glorious. The time of temptation had been nothing short of horrible. To experience the delusion and power of temptation that Our created man endured his whole life caused compassion to well up in My heart. One day My followers would receive greater power by Holy Spirit.

Satan was limited but so sly and cunning in his deceptive practices and destruction upon humanity. I remembered his ruse eons ago when he even corrupted the loyalty of a third of the heavenly host.

I had struggled with temptation and the pull of sin, as it was necessary for the Son of Man. In My victory over temptation, by the empowerment of Holy Spirit and the weaponry of the Word of God, I established the example to be followed by My disciples until the end of this age.

The next task at hand was a big transition in My earthly life. The ministry outlined by FATHER would soon begin. It would begin slowly and increase. In the days ahead, I would begin to gather My disciples; the faces in My dream would come into full view. I knew they would be from an unlikely lot. They would be as surprised by My call as their families and friends. None would feel worthy or competent, which would be their first qualification for service.

Some would be quiet and reserved. Others would be loud and boisterous. Some would be meditative and careful. Others would be presumptuous and careless. Most would be common laborers, while a few would be rich.

All but one would ultimately be faithful and loyal. Each one on our journey together would experience fear, failure, doubt, and disappointment. They were ordinary men who would follow the Messiah, sometimes stumbling and sometimes soaring. They would be the seedstock of faith that would be sown in the soil of the earth, putting forth shoots of growth that would eventually encompass the whole world with the message of salvation and power.

CHAPTER TWELVE

UP FROM
THE WILDERNESS

Behold! The Lamb of God who takes away the sin of the world!
JOHN 1:29

My journey out of the wilderness that first evening was made mostly in solitude. I made good time and covered a good distance, but soon the sun would set. I found a rock outcropping at the base of a hill that would make a good shelter for the night. It was the season of fruit, and I had gathered a supper's worth of various kinds on My way. I lay on My mat, peering into the starry night with great comfort and peace. I was thankful to be on the next leg of My journey.

The next day's travel brought Me into more settled areas. I began to encounter a few people. As I traveled past small houses built of wood and thatch, it was interesting to see the reaction of the adults. Some ventured a greeting, while others ignored My presence. It made Me consider how the unseen and unloved felt. Many people felt that God did not see or care for them. The presence of the Son of God among men was God's journey on earth. Some would never see Me as such.

My load was light as I traveled. In My knapsack were only a few items. I had a good shard of flint and a small piece of iron for kindling a fire with a spark. I usually had a small piece of pitch wood for a little kindling on the nights when everything was damp. Also in My bag was a spare tunic and a spare linen garment as My only extra clothing.

Ima had insisted I take a small earthen cooking vessel. She had taught Me to forage from the land when I was a boy, so I knew the edible plants in the countryside. A wild leek could add some flavor to a salt-cured fish, or the leaves of a saltbush could be cooked with an egg. The Torah allowed for a traveler to glean fruit or grains to eat on a journey, but they could not be put in a carrying vessel or be harvested with a sickle.

I usually carried a woven wool sleeping mat about twice the thickness of a blanket, plus a wool blanket made by My grandmother. I rolled them both into a tight bundle and tied it with braided twine, leaving a loop so I could drape it over My shoulder. Sometimes on these treks from one place to another, in desolate places, I often slept under a tree. My mat protected Me from the cool ground, and My blanket and cloak warmed Me from the night air.

I had little attachment to anything on this earth, knowing I was a sojourner and not a settler. FATHER had revealed My purpose, journey, and destination. The principle of value I held in My heart was not in the items that fire could destroy or thieves could steal but rather in the true treasures of eternity. These things I would teach to My followers.

Before I left Nazareth, I had emptied My hands of most things I had accumulated in My thirty years. I gave all My tools and extra clothes to My brothers. The other things I had collected were given to My precious sisters. In preparation of My leaving, I had made each of them a gift of a small wooden chest. I cherished even today the sound of their squeals of delight when I presented their gifts.

Ima had received all the silver and copper in My money pouch the day before I left. When I emptied the coins onto the table, she had urged Me to keep the money. I had explained how FATHER fed the birds every day and told her all My needs would be provided for from His hand. She had only smiled and put the coins into her leather pouch.

On the day of My departure, when I had reached the edge of Nazareth, a dear neighbor had pressed a few coins into My hand while giving Me a prayer of blessing. He had looked deep into My eyes while still holding a firm grip and said, "You were always different than all the other boys. I do not know what You will do in this world, but I know Adonai's hand is on Your life. I wanted to be the first to give You some oil for the lamp with which You will bring light to this dark world. Shalom, my son."

He had pulled Me close and kissed My cheek as tears flowed down his weathered face. He never would have believed it, but on that day, he had spoken as a prophet.

The one treasure from My youth was a small knife that I cherished. The blade was about a handbreadth in length. It was so treasured because My grandfather on Ima's side of the family gave it to Me when I entered manhood. I smiled when I thought of his simple words: "Now that you are a man, you need a good knife." Abba had helped Me fashion a sheath for it from some tanned cowhide.

The knife was treasured, although I knew it would not be Mine forever. It would be handed to one of My disciples on a very solemn night. It was a token of My grandfather's love, as well as a reminder that all earthly treasures were eventually left behind. The true treasures were sent heavenward and lasted forever, while the things of earth turned back to dust or vapors from a fire.

While I journeyed toward Galilee, I was thinking forward. There were some men who at that very moment were going about their daily lives with no understanding of the events about to unfold for them. The fishermen were mending their nets, a few men were following John the Baptizer, a tax collector was counting his proceeds, a zealot was conspiring terror, and others were buying goods in the market.

A tear ran down My cheek as I visualized a woman from Magdala who was presently being tormented by seven demons and thinking her life was ruined and wasted. I would not search for her or the others, but FATHER's hand would guide their steps and Mine until we were face-to-face.

None of these people would seem to be the obvious choice. They were like the young shepherd David, who was guarding the sheep while his brothers were invited to the sacrifice of Samuel the prophet. God directed Samuel to reject all the invited but call for the one not welcomed.

The invited of My days were the priests, the Levites, the Pharisees, and the Sadducees. These were the leaders of our faith. Their doubt would disqualify themselves, but the outcasts would become My chosen.

As I pondered those who would follow Me, I came to a small village as the sun began to melt into the western horizon. A man was gathering a few figs from his tree while his wife cooked some bread on a rounded stone heated by hot coals. He looked up and called to Me, "Shalom, stranger. Do you have a place to lay your head tonight?"

"Shalom, My friend. Only if you have space for My mat. If not, under a terebinth tree just over the next knoll," I answered. "If you could spare a handful of figs, I would be thankful to glean some from your tree. It would be a blessing to Me."

He smiled. "Oh, my friend, we have more than a handful of

figs. We have bread, oil with herbs to dip it in, dried fish, and all the figs you desire. And of course, a place for your mat."

"Thank you so much! I accept your kindness. May Adonai's blessings be on your house for your hospitality and kindness."

After I washed My feet, cooled My face, and rinsed My hands, we retired inside their house. Ethan and Eliana's home was typical of these parts, with a main room and two small rooms. I was expecting children to be in the yard playing, but there were none.

We ate our meal, and it was very good, surpassed only by the angels' portion after My long fast. The meal reminded Me of Ima's food. It satisfied My hunger and brought memories of My mother. I missed her greatly! I was hoping for a visit with her on My return to Galilee.

When supper ended, Ethan spoke with Me like we were longtime friends; he was very open in his conversation. He had the same number of years as Me, and his wife was five years younger. It had been almost ten years since they were married, and still they had no children. Eliana was barren. She shamefully lowered her eyes as her husband explained the absence of children. I sensed her humiliation, as was common with the barren women of our people. My heart swelled with compassion for them, especially for her.

Ethan led Me to My room, and I unrolled My mat. I was thankful for the kindness of My newfound friends. I pulled off My cloak and hung it to air on the back of door. My tired body melted into the mat. But the fatigue did not deter Me from My nightly prayer and a special prayer for Ethan and Eliana. Sleep came suddenly and deeply.

Before I knew it, morning was being declared by a neighbor's rooster and the dim light of dawn filtering through My window. I stretched and rose to begin another day of My journey. Eliana had been up long enough to have an egg cooked with succulent greens, which topped some leftover bread.

I filled My water jug from some of their water jars, gathered My things, and was ready to depart. Then the Holy Spirit began to stir in Me an abounding compassion for Eliana.

They were busy about their morning duties, and I was about to call for them when Ethan came up. He said, "Here are some figs for Your trip. Is there something more we can do for Your journey?"

"Thank you so much for the sweet figs. No. I need nothing else. You both have been wonderful hosts, and I thank you for your kindness."

Ethan, the gracious host, answered, "It has been our pleasure, not a burden."

Looking to his wife, I said, "Eliana, do you know what your name means?"

She replied, "Yes. If I remember, it means, 'God has answered.'"

"Yes, you remember correctly. I know you have asked Adonai for a child. It is the one prayer you have prayed every day. So I tell you, daughter of Adonai, He has answered your prayers. There will be a baby's cry heard in this home before one year has passed, and God will grant you a son, who will fulfill all your desires when you are old and tell many others of Adonai's love."

Eliana and Ethan began to weep tears of faith and gratitude. She fell and kissed My feet. Through her sobbing, she said, "Jesus, we will never forget your name."

I took her hand, lifted her up, and then, looking at them both, declared, "Neither will your son!"

They walked with Me to the edge of the village. I looked back to see them embracing and still looking My way as I topped the little knoll. Soon I disappeared from their view. A strong urge of FATHER pulled Me toward Galilee. There would be just a few brief encounters along the way. In My soul, I rejoiced in the healing of Eliana's womb and for her coming son, who one day would preach My Gospel after I had gone from earth.

My journey led Me through the area with Jerusalem to the west and the Dead Sea to the east. I would not be going into the city of Jerusalem today because My people of destiny were in the land of Galilee.

Passing by Jerusalem, I could see the walls and buildings in the distance. This was a city of great destiny for Me in FATHER's purpose, yet today the city was bypassed by the Messiah. In My mind, I saw the Pharisees and scribes scurrying about in their self-absorbed importance, dressed in long robes and wearing phylacteries on their foreheads. They had no idea the Messiah was passing them by for the fishermen and other common folk of Galilee. When I thought about it, it made Me chuckle at the absurdity of it all, but I also felt the sorrow for their error of arrogant blindness.

I had about a week's worth of travel before I would reach My destination of Galilee. Capernaum would become My station of ministry.

Since I had left the Jordan after John's baptism, I'd had very little contact with people except for a few villagers. I loved people, but solitude was a reprieve for Me to be alone with FATHER and Holy Spirit.

When I came to Jericho, I turned east and crossed the Jordan River to the place of My baptism by John. I remembered his abandoned look as I left him and headed to the Judean wilderness. He had been confused because the long-awaited Messiah was going away from him. Now I was coming back.

As I approached, He shouted with a loud, happy voice: "Behold! The Lamb of God who takes away the sin of the world! This is He of whom I said, 'After me comes a Man who is preferred before me, for He was before me.' I did not know Him; but that He should be revealed to Israel, therefore I came baptizing with water" (John 1:29–31).

His strong declaration resulted in strange stares from most around him, but on a few of his disciples' faces were excited smiles. After the crowd dispersed, John and I talked. He was confused at why I left so quickly without explanation nearly two months ago. He had not heard anything about My whereabouts or My activities. He questioned, "Where have you been?"

Smiling at his brash nature, I briefly explained about My time in the Judean wilderness. He was very attentive when I told of FATHER's impartation and the awful temptation of the evil one. I told him about the greater revealed purpose of FATHER and My mission going forward. There were many things I could not tell him, but I spoke enough to explain My absence and some of My future. I spent the night on the banks of the Jordan in a nice clump of small trees with his encampment.

The next morning before daylight, I slipped away from the others to pray. I needed this time with FATHER as I prepared for My time of ministry and the gathering of My disciples. When My prayer time was finished, the others had risen for the day.

Upon returning to the encampment, I saw John standing with two of his disciples. He looked at Me as I approached, and I heard him repeat his previous proclamation, "Behold! The Lamb of God who takes away the sin of the world!" (John 1:36).

I saw his two disciples look at John, look My way, and then whisper to each other.

When I walked up to John, His disciples gave us some space. We spoke briefly. I told him all I needed to say, because I knew this would be My last time to see him in this realm. My ministry was about to begin, and his was about to end. We said our goodbyes. John was smiling, while My heart was gripped with sadness. He was of the greatest among prophets. Even as babies in the womb, the Spirit of God had connected us. The things I knew about his death and mine I would not disclose to him.

With a hearty "shalom" to John and his disciples, I continued My journey to Galilee. I was one hour into My journey when I looked back and saw two familiar faces intently following. They were the two disciples of John. Stepping under the shade of a tree, I waited for them to catch up.

I asked them what they were seeking. They answered, "Teacher, where are you staying?" (John 1:38). Their names were Andrew and John the son of Zebedee. I knew them to be fishermen from Bethsaida and partners. They each had a fisherman brother. John's father was also among the partners.

I told them to come and see where I was staying if they were interested. They stayed with Me that first day and asked many questions. The next day they left but said they would return.

I knew Andrew and John were humble men. They were introspective types, unlike their former teacher, John the Baptist, who was loud and bold.

When they returned, Andrew was accompanied by his brother Simon. Even though Simon was not a disciple of John the Baptist, he was much like him in his demeanor. It was easy to see that Simon had a forceful personality. He would be like a bull that needed a firm hand to lead. He was strong as a stone and just as immovable.

We greeted each other, and then I renamed him Cephas, which also translated into Peter, meaning a stone. He was rock-hard and just as stubborn. I smiled in My mind, remembering how Abba had taught Me to chisel stones.

He smiled and, with a smirky glance toward Andrew, said, "Well, Rabbi, you know me already, huh?" He was not yet ready to follow. Andrew had pestered him to come.

I granted him no answer. Then I quietly groaned in My soul while thinking, *He will be great, but I have much work to do in carving this jagged stone into a disciple.*

The number of disciples began to grow, but they still looked like a band of vagabonds wandering about, not knowing their purpose. The next day, I found Philip, who lived in Bethsaida, the same city of Simon and Andrew. He willingly fell in behind us when I simply told him to follow Me. He was a likable sort with a broad smile.

Philip's soul was a deep well that bubbled up fresh water. He was excited to begin this discipleship journey and soon found Nathanael, sometimes called Bartholomew. Philip told Me later that Nathanael was surprised to think the Messiah would come from Nazareth, the little ridiculed town in Galilee. Philip told him, "You must come and see for yourself."

When I saw Nathanael coming to join us, I saw that his heart was honest and open. I told him that he was an Israelite with no deceit. Nathanael was further astonished when I told him I had seen him under the shade of a fig tree.

The joy of his gentle soul burst out: "Oh, Teacher. Yes, You are the Messiah, the Son of God! The King who is to come!"

"Nathanael, just because I told you where you were, do you believe? There will be much greater things that your eyes will see. From now on, you will see heaven open and angels rising and coming down on Me."

His face shown as brightly as if he were an angel on earth.

I turned and began to walk down the road toward Capernaum, where I was going to stay. Philip had arranged a spacious house for Me, owned by a kind and generous man who was his kindred. Capernaum was a good location; it was located near the Sea of Galilee, giving us an opportunity to travel often by boat.

Looking back, I saw Andrew, John, Philip, and Nathanael,

with Simon reluctantly tagging along. All but Simon looked excited. But they were also anxious over what was next.

When we arrived in Capernaum, I told them they could stay with Me, or if they needed a few days to take care of some things it was not a problem. My preaching would begin gradually. We would work for about two weeks in Capernaum beginning in the local synagogue and local marketplace. Afterwards, I would need to go to Nazareth and then to Cana for My youngest sister Adina's wedding. After the wedding, we would return to Capernaum and the ministry will become more intense. If they were to be My disciples, they were to be totally committed and follow Me.

It was necessary for Me to return to Nazareth. One principle my disciples needed to understand that you start where you are. I was from Nazareth. Yes, I wanted to check on My mother and kindred, but most importantly, there was a step of ministry I needed to take in Nazareth.

Philip and Nathanael agreed to stay with Me. Andrew and John said they needed to go back to Bethsaida with Simon, but would return in a few days.

Simon shrugged; he was not yet convinced. The seed had been planted in him, but it had not yet sprouted in his heart. He was to be a rock; for now, he was just stone cold and hard.

Two days later, Andrew and John rejoined us, and we began at the synagogue in Capernaum. I was invited to read from the scroll and speak about the scripture. I read from the scroll that contained the *Shema* (Deut. 6:4-9). My teaching was centered on the FATHER's command to love Him with all our heart, soul, and strength. The people's attention was fixed upon Me as I spoke. I felt the power of the Spirit. Afterwards, many of the people said My words were powerful and filled with life, unlike the dull teaching of the scribes.

The next day a small group of people found their way to the

house where I was staying. They were very intrigued by the power in My words and wanted to know more. I invited them into the little courtyard behind the house under the shade of a tree. I spoke to them about the kingdom of God being present in power to bring salvation and wholeness.

It was fresh words to their weary souls and most soaked in My teaching as water clings to a hyssop branch. When My talk came to an end they lingered with a weight of expectation. I was moved with compassion for them, seeing their needs and sensing their faith.

There was a man with a limp caused by a broken bone improperly healed. I asked him if he wanted to be made whole.

He hobbled to Me without saying a word with the sparkle in his eyes saying, *yes*. I touched his leg and then looking intently at him, I declared, "Son of Abraham, receive by faith the healing in your leg."

I saw the joyous look on his face when his leg became whole. He took two steps with no limp and tears of joy flowed from his eyes! He exclaimed, "Oh dear Rabbi, You have healed my crippled leg. I have limped since I was teenager. Thank you! Praise Adonai!"

Then others came for My touch. One came with a stiff neck unable to turn to the right or left. After his healing, he could not stop moving his head with amazement. A young lady brought her two-year-old daughter who had not yet walked. Everyone was almost excited as the mother when the child was running and skipping with new-found strength.

They were all amazed and excited, as were My four disciples. It took Me a few minutes to calm them so I could warn them. "My friends, please listen to Me. I praise Adonai with you for the wholeness you have received. But please, I ask you to keep this good news to yourself. We are not fully ready to begin our public ministry here in Capernaum, Bethsaida, and the surrounding area. I will soon be leaving for Nazareth, but I will return to preach and to do God's work. So, please bear with My request to keep this good news quiet for now."

They looked puzzled but agreed and kissed My hand as they left full of joy.

Soon, the healings and the healing prophet became the news of Capernaum, even though few had witnessed the healings. Travelers who went out from Capernaum spread the news in many parts, including Nazareth.

My initial teaching and healing, in My private yard, were with a few people. It was a meager beginning compared to the soon blossoming ministry in Galilee.

Soon, it was time for our trek to Nazareth. Along the way, we had many good discussions about the kingdom of God. My four disciples were eager students. They were a willing group, and their thirst for understanding was like an unwritten scroll for a scribe to write on.

When we entered the outer edges of Nazareth, there was quite a stir as My neighbors came out of their doors, calling, "Hey, everyone, Jesus has returned!" When we were close to Ima's home, her house emptied of My kindred. Ima was smiling, and My precious sisters were trilling pure joy with their tongues. We hugged and laughed. It was a great reunion, and they were full of questions about My months away.

My former home looked strangely different. No, the walls and roof were all the same. It was like a dream of a familiar place yet also strange. This was where I had grown to adulthood. In this house was where I had closed the eyes of Abba when he died. It was once My home but not My home anymore. When I was a boy, My life had been mostly defined by this place, but now the world awaited, and FATHER's purpose was My meaning.

Ima welcomed My traveling disciples with her usual hospitality. She was excited to see that I had gathered four disciples so soon. There was an instant connection between My mother and My disciples, especially John. Within an hour, the five seemed like they had known each other forever.

After a nice supper, we talked. Ima became serious and said, "News of your healing miracles have reached the ears of Nazareth. Many do not know what to think about the hometown healing prophet whom they knew as a boy."

I smiled and said, "Ima, it is amazing how fast the news traveled. I had only a small group in a private place where I ministered to them. They were warned to keep silent of the things they had experienced, but it is difficult for people to hold their tongues. Our ministry will grow in strength when we return to Capernaum. I only have four disciples, but others will join Me soon."

She questioned Me, "Tomorrow is the Sabbath. I am sure the local leader will want You to read from the scroll, and then add your thoughts. Are you ready to preach?"

"Yes, Ima! I look forward to the reading of the scroll. FATHER and Holy Spirit have revealed to Me the text that has been chosen and the words that will follow."

Ima had become comfortable with Me speaking of FATHER, but My mention of Holy Spirit in such a familiar way caused a questioning look on her face. She said nothing, but she sensed the deepening of My spiritual journey even though it was now strange to her.

I knew the men in tomorrow's synagogue gathering had known Me as a boy and then as an apprentice carpenter. Their familiarity with Me would cloud their minds and cause them to not receive My words. FATHER had shown Me that My teaching and ministry would bring many to understanding, but many more would resist My words.

I asked My mother, "Ima, are you ready for tomorrow?"

My question was awkward for her. "Yes," she answered. "I am always excited to hear you speak. Your new journey of life leaves me unsure of many things, but Adonai will help us. I am always concerned about You." She laughed. "I am still Your mother, you know!"

I smiled to reassure her concerns. "Yes, Ima, you will always be My beloved mother. I love you beyond words can describe. One of My great concerns is how My life going forward will affect you. I must do as FATHER directs, but I also pray every day for your strength and courage. We both recall old Simeon's words in the temple when I was so small."

Ima gave a weary smile and exclaimed, "Oh yes! How could I ever forget his words about a sword piercing my heart." She had always been unsure of the meaning of Simeon's words. Unbeknown to her, the sword of which he spoke would soon be unsheathed, but its actual piercing would come in the years ahead.

Yes, I also knew the *Sword of the Spirit* was about to be unsheathed in Nazareth. My journey as the Messiah had begun, and I would be revealed to many in Israel and even to the Gentiles of the earth. There would be many who heard. Not all would believe, but to those who believed in Me, life would come and living water would flow forth.

I stepped outside and scanned the village from the front of Ima's house. This was My childhood home from the time we had come from Egypt. I looked toward the edge of the village to the well where we drew water. I glanced toward the hill where I had become awakened to My reality as Messiah. Then I looked toward the synagogue where I would read from the scroll in the morning.

I was alone on the village road, but I was filled with the Holy

Spirit and sensed the presence of FATHER. I inhaled a fresh breath of air and then exhaled it out while declaring with My lips, "The Spirit of the LORD is upon Me" (Luke 4:18).

Tomorrow, the synagogue!

Printed in the United States
by Baker & Taylor Publisher Services